To my boys, Dean and Joe, for being the inspiration behind the birth of this story, and without whom it would never have been born.

PLAYING MUM

Death is only the beginning…

A novella by Elizabeth Coffey

© 2019 Elizabeth Coffey. All rights reserved.

SEVEN YEARS EARLIER

It was a cold and blustery November afternoon. Autumn leaves danced amongst the headstones in the church grounds. People gathered around the open grave. Pam, gripped hands with her seven-year-old son. A big baby bump protruded from her slender body. The wind picked up pace, whipping her long silky dark brown hair across her face as she threw a single rose into the hole. Her son held a childish drawing of himself, riding a scooter with one leg out, the way his father taught him. He turned to his mother. She squeezed her worried little boy's hand gently and winked,

"Don't be scared, Harry, be strong."

Hands shaking, he dropped the drawing; it fluttered deep into the hole. The priest waited, then crossed his heart and threw a handful of dirt on top of the coffin.

"Let us commend unto the mercy of God, Joshua Harry..." his voice trailed off.

Creepy Carl edged closer to Pam. His dark wavy mullet defying the laws of gravity with equal contempt. His face like a mask, controlled, in order to have a particular effect on her. It doesn't. Pam stood firm, pulling her black wool coat a little tighter around her body. She waited until the priest had finished his prayer, then took the boy's hand and walked away from the hostile crowd. Creepy Carl followed. He grabbed her by the arm, Pam yanked it away, bent down to her son and whispered,

"Harry, be a good boy, go and wait by the car for Mummy."

Harry did as he was told. As soon as he was out of earshot Pam turned to face creepy Carl.

"I don't want to talk to you, not here, not ever, show some respect for your brother, will you?"

"Why should I?" he growled. "He never showed me any, you turned him against me."

"You did that yourself, Carl. You poisoned your family against *me* with your twisted lies, but your brother saw straight through you."

He leant into Pam, so close, she could feel his warm cigarette breath on her cheek. "It doesn't have to be like this, me and you…"

"There is no me and you, there never was, and there never will be. You're not half the man Josh was. In fact, what are you?" Pam eyed him up and down. "Five, eight, bit less, maybe?"

"Then you better start packing," he sneered.

"Over my dead body. I will fight you all the way, not for me, for Josh's children…ouch!"

Pam grabbed her tummy, stooped forward and fell to the ground.

"MUMMY! NO! Harry raced across the grass, tripping and falling.

CHAPTER ONE

HORRIBLE UGLY LITTLE MAN

Fourteen-year-old Harry, dressed up in an oversized leather jacket and a giant pair of sunglasses towered over his seven-year-old brother holding a bottle of tomato ketchup. Josh, also sporting a leather jacket and a long brown wig, fell to the ground playing dead. From a great height, Harry dribbled sauce onto his brother's face. A distant female voice called out,

"Harry! Joshua! Come in now, boys!"

Back from the dead, Josh, stared at his brother wide-eyed. "Oh no, what are we going to do?"

"Quick, wipe it off," said Harry, pouring more on his little brother's face at the same time.

"Harry! You've got some on Mum's hair!"

"You look gay in that wig, by the way."

"No, I don't! I look like a Hells Angel." Josh frowned, frantically wiping off the sauce with his bare hands onto the grass.

Quick-thinking Harry, stuffed his mum's Gucci sunglasses into his pocket, ready to sneak them back into her handbag later. "Come on, buddy, last one indoors is a rotten egg." He ran off in slow-motion.

"Not fair! You're faster than me!" Josh scrambled to his feet, running as fast as his little legs could carry him, he overtook his brother. "Ha, ha, Harry, you're a rotten egg!" He laughed, triumphantly.

***

Pam was head down, singing happily and packing stuff into cardboard boxes. Her once cozy bedroom was now sparse and unhomely, but she didn't care. Nothing could take away the joy of moving far, far, away. She turned around to greet the boys, her smile vanished. Both their jackets were covered in mud and grass stains. Josh's face was tinged red from ketchup, the wig ruffled.

"Where did you get those jackets from? And my wig…"

Harry pointed to an open box in the corner of the room.

"Put those things back now! You've ruined your dad's bike leathers! Look at you, Josh you're caked in mud, and tomato sauce? For God's sake!"

She grabbed hold of him, wrestled the jacket off, Frisbee'd it into a box, then yanked the wig off his head.

"It was his fault." Josh pointed at Harry.

"My fault? You're the one that wanted to play Terminator!"

Pam sighed, exasperated. "Never mind, stop arguing, put the jacket back in the box, Harry."

Moody Harry took the jacket off and put it back in the box, purposefully bashing into Josh as he walked past him. Josh lashed out and missed.

"You took them out of the box, Harry!" he shouted.

"Yeah well, it was your dumb-arse idea to use ketchup," Harry retaliated.

"No, it wasn't!"

"Yes, it was, you lying little ponce, you're such a grass."

Harry pulled back a fist ready to punch. Josh put an arm up in defense.

"STOP IT! THE PAIR OF YOU! YOU'RE DRIVING ME INSANE!"

It came out louder than it should have in the echoey room, but it had the desired effect. The boys froze. Harry slowly lowered his clenched fist. Frustrated, Pam counted silently to five on her fingers, then calmly spoke.

"Boys, I'm sorry, I don't mind you playing with them, I'm a bit stressed that's all, ask me first next time, please?" She reached out towards them, begrudgingly the boys group hugged.

"Mum what was it like being a Hells Angel when you were young?" Josh asked.

"A Hells Angel? Why do you say that?"

Josh pointed at the ruffled wig his mum was still holding.

"Oh, the wig." She laughed. "I wasn't a Hells Angel."

"HA-RRY! He said that was your hair from when you were a Hells Angel. Liar!"

Harry looked at his mum, indignant. "You were. That's why you bought the wig, you said."

"A Hell's Angel..." Pam chuckled at her teenage son's – remembered slightly wrong – memory. "I was a punk. I bought this wig to cover up my pink spiky hair when I went to work."

"Oh yeah... a punk." Harry's face turned red.

Josh pointed a finger at his brother, mocking him. "Ha, ha, Harry."

Straight-faced, Harry poked his tongue out and flipped Josh the finger.

"Right, boys, enough! Time to pack, honestly, your rooms look like the mess-fairies have been in there." Pam gestured to the stack of empty boxes under the windowsill. "Go on, off you go, chop-chop."

Josh raced over, grabbed the biggest box and darted off to his bedroom. Harry, on the other hand meandered across the room, dragging his feet, hoping to get her attention. He thought she hadn't noticed. He picked up an empty box and headed off to his room.

"Everything okay, Harry?"

Harry stopped in the doorway. "Mum, I don't want to go."

Seeing her son's sorrowful expression, Pam's tense mood softened. "Aw Harry, please don't be sad, it'll make me sad."

"It's because of Uncle Carl, isn't it? I'm not stupid, I read the solicitors letter on the kitchen table. Why is he doing this to us? I don't understand."

"You're old enough to understand, so if you really want to know, I'll tell you."

"I really want to know."

Pam peered through the door, Josh was happily packing in his room, pushing the door to –slightly, she plopped down onto the bed, patting the duvet for Harry to sit next to her. She lowered her voice. "Uncle Carl and your father bought this house to make money."

"What… you mean, it's not our home?"

"Of course it is, darling, they had an agreement. We would live in it and look after it and when you grew up they would sell it and split the money, but then they fell out, and when your dad died, Uncle Carl tried to take all of it."

"Did he? What an arse."

"Language, Timothy! Yes, he did, but the court said no, he can only have half, as per the agreement."

"Hah! Good!"

"It is good, but that's why we have to sell, to give him his half. To be honest, I'll be glad to see the back of this house, Harry, and him, I've been fighting this battle for seven years."

"I hate Uncle Carl. I remember at Dad's funeral, I saw him hit you."

"Hit me? What makes you say that?"

"I saw it, when you fell to the ground."

"Oh, sweetheart, he didn't hit me. I had a massive contraction. Your little brother knocked me off my feet."

"I still think he's a horrible ugly little man."

Pam laughed. "Funny boy." She ruffled his hair and kissed him on the forehead. "Creepy Carl and his horrible family will never find us. You'll have a better life, I promise."

Two beefy men jumped out of the removal lorry and started unloading. Pam pulled up behind – outside her wonderful new home. Well, that's how she had described it to the boys. Without the rose tinted specs it was a dilapidated grey cottage, in the middle of nowhere, it seemed. Nestling away in its overgrown grass and bedraggled rosebushes, desperately in need of a good paint. The boys were unusually quiet in the back of the car, not a good sign. Secretly, Pam wondered if this was the biggest mistake of all time.

"Mum, is this *really* our new home…" Harry pointed to the SOLD board.

"Listen, Harry, I know it looks terrible at the moment, but…"

"Wow! That is awesome!"

"It's a castle!" Exclaimed Josh.

The boys leapt out of the car and shot off. Pam crossed her heart and blew a kiss into the sky. Grabbing armfuls of stuff off the passenger seat and carefully balancing her chin on top of the wobbling pile, she headed precariously to the house.

***

Harry clambered through the brambles and climbed over the broken fence into the back garden. Josh trailed behind. "I'm going this way," he said, darting off to investigate.

"That way's boring!" Harry called out.

"Want to bet!" Josh shouted, running off in the direction of a ginormous earth mound. Harry hadn't seen it, he was transfixed, looking down at something unusual.

"Hey, Harry! *You're a dirty rascal!*" Josh sang loudly.

Harry looked up and saw Josh on top of the ginormous earth mound, spying on him from his elevated viewpoint, at the boring end of the garden.

"Josh! Quick come over here!"

It seemed to be some kind of wall in the ground. Intrigued, Harry bent down, digging with his bare hands at the overgrown grass and mud surrounding the bricks until he exposed a metal lid. Ha, it didn't take long for his partner in crime to appear and start bogging over his shoulder. Harry yanked at the handle. Once, twice, third time lucky, the lid came away revealing a big dark opening.

"Whoa, look at that, Josh!"

"What is it?"

"It looks like some sort of hideout, maybe from the war or something."

"Get in it, Harry, go on, dare you."

"You get in first, I'll help you then you can help me, yeah?" said Harry, knowing full well his little brother would jump off a cliff if he told him to. Josh slithered down into the hideout. Harry closed the lid, grinning to himself.

"HEY! LET ME OUT!" said a muffled voice.

"I'll come back for you after dinner, bye muppet."

Mimicking footsteps, Harry banged his fists repeatedly on the ground.

"MUMMY! HELP!" the panic-stricken muffled voice hollered.

Harry opened the lid. "Joking, muppet! Jeez, don't be such a baby."

"Get me out of here, it's too dark, I don't like it," Josh whimpered.

"Move out the way, Josh, I'm coming in."

Harry slid into the pitch-black hole. He switched on the torch function of his iPhone, flashing the light around, his eyes wild with excitement. "Man, this is wicked!" Josh stopped whimpering and cuffed his watery eyes. "It can be our secret den."

"Boys! Where are you?" a distant voice called out.

"Come on, Josh, let's go."

Harry pushed Josh up and out of the hole. Josh, helped Harry climb out. He replaced the lid carefully and gleamed at Josh. "I reckon we should come back at nighttime, or are you too scared?"

"I'm not scared!"

"You in, brother?"

Harry held his hand up to Josh, they high fived then performed their special handshake.

"I'm in, brother."

Harry scraped the mud back over the lid and ran off with Josh trailing behind. "Rotten egg!"

***

The boys sat either side of Pam at the big oak desk, waiting for the headmaster. She glanced around the room, admiring the vast collage of children's drawings of aliens and planets that adorned most of the walls. Harry jabbed Josh in the side; squelching fart sounds emanated from his coat pocket. Josh whooped with uncontrollable laughter.

"Stop it, boys, Professor Evans will be here any minute."

Harry gave her an evil grin. "You woke me up with a wet flannel on my face."

"What's that got to do with anything?" She rolled her eyes.

"I don't care what Professor Evans thinks, that's what," said a defiant Harry.

"We'll see." She smiled, knowingly.

The door creaked open. Pam gave Harry *that* look and he yanked his hand out of his pocket. She poked Josh in the belly, he stopped mid-whoop. An elderly gentleman, with gold-rimmed spectacles and a long cloak like something out of Harry Potter, hobbled into the room. His once thick curly brown hair now grey and wispy, sprouted from the top of his balding head. His steely grey-blue eyes displaying that familiar air of authority, almost rebelling against his stooping body. He had aged, a lot. Like a naughty child, Pam leapt up out of her chair, the boys copied.

"Talking about me?" The stern-faced professor made a beeline for Harry, stopping two inches away and scrutinising his face. "Farting pot, eh, I used to have one of those, you must be Harry?"

"He... Hello sir, no it's not a farting pot actually, it's my iPhone, sir."

Josh giggled. Pam elbowed him in the ribs. The professor held out his hand. Pam cringed as Harry took the iPhone out of his pocket and handed it over.

"Hmm," said the professor, inspecting the phone as if it were something from the year 2050. He handed it back to Harry, his staid expression morphing into that cheesy grin Pam remembered so well. He boldly shook Harry's lettuce leaf hand. "Silly me, times have changed somewhat."

Next, the professor turned his scrutiny to Josh. "Sense of humour, eh? I used to have one of those too. You must be Josh. Pleased to meet you, young man."

Beaming from ear to ear, Josh shook his hand robustly. "I've got a farting pot!"

"Jolly good fun, aren't they, especially in restaurants." The Professor winked at Josh then turned to Pam, he grabbed her outstretched hand with both of his and shook it vigorously.

"Professor, I'm so sorry..." she apologised.

"No need, Mrs Jones, they seem very normal boys to me. Shall we?"

Pam, and her boys, followed the professor to the door. A pretty girl, slim, her blonde hair tugged back into a neat ponytail, around the same age as Harry she guessed, was waiting in the corridor.

"Holley, this little fellow is Josh, take him to Mrs Morgan then take Harry to Miss Allen's class with you."

"Yes, sir," Holley replied, pulling her sagging over-knee socks back up over her knees where they belonged and turning slightly pink. Feeling nervous on their behalf, Pam thanked the girl and gave the boys a quick hug as they ventured off. "Have a good day," she called after them.

Professor Evans closed the door and escorted a concerned looking Pam back to the desk. "They're in good hands, Mrs Jones." He smiled. "Please, have a seat." Ever the gentleman he pulled out the chair for her and handed her a form and a pen. "All you need to do is fill out this form and we're done."

"Oh." Pam sat down and stared at the form, her face troubled. "I can't."

"Yes, you can, it's easy, you hold the pen like this, you put it on the paper like this…" he demonstrated.

"Professor Evans I don't have a next of kin."

The professor lowered his gold-rimmed glasses. "I understand you lost your husband some years ago, but, you have no other next of kin? No parents?"

"My parents are dead."

The professor's baffled expression softened. "Mrs Jones, forgive me, I had no idea…"

"It was a long time ago. My parents were killed in a car crash when I was fourteen. A week after I left this school actually… Jammy-Pammy ring any bells?"

"Jammy-Pammy! The girl who brought…"

"Jam sandwiches to school every day." Pam chuckled.

"Goodness me." The professor was taken aback. "I can see it now," he smiled. "If it wasn't for that mole on your lip right there, I would never have guessed… wait a minute, don't you have a little sister?"

"I do, in Australia somewhere, God knows where mind, all I've got is an old photograph."

"I'm so sorry to hear that." The professor looked genuinely sad.

"Haunts me to this day, the way she cried when they dragged her away. She was only seven. I promised her that, no matter what happens to us, wherever we are, we will find each other…" Pam stopped, too choked to continue.

The professor leant across the desk and put a hand on hers. "No success I take it?"

"No, Australia's a big place, that's partly the reason I came back here, in the hope she might find me, I have a strange gut feeling about it."

"And your late husband, doesn't he have…"

"No." Pam answered, a little too abruptly. "He doesn't, it's just me and the boys, they're all I've got and I'm all they've got."

The professor was speechless. "Mrs Jones – Pammy, I hate to say this, but have you ever thought about… God forbid… if something happened to you?"

"Yes, Professor Evans, I have."

"And I'm sure nothing will." The professor smiled. "Good to have you back, Jammy Pammy."

CHAPTER TWO

DEATH IS ONLY THE BEGINNING

Paige stared at herself in the ugly mirror. Her face was gaunt and tired. Her short silky dark brown hair, dull as ditchwater. Never mind thirty-three, she looked more like a hundred and three. Any minute now the consultant would be coming to discharge her and she couldn't wait. Comfy as it was – private hospitals always give you three pillows, her friend told her, and she was right – nothing could compare to her magnificent white beach house snuggled amongst the rocks and dunes on Australia's Gold Coast.

Mr Gangulu popped his head around the curtain and waved. Paige propped herself up on her trio of pillows while the consultant perched himself on the edge of the bed, next to her tatty fluffy owl.

"I'm sorry you will never be able to have children, Miss Edwards – Paige, if I may, but if it hadn't have been for the hysterectomy this heart condition may never have been discovered."

"I can't have kids but I'm lucky to be alive, right?"

Mr Gangulu explained that the CT scan showed an unusual heartbeat during the operation. It revealed an aneurysm in her aorta which was about to erupt at any moment. Death would have been imminent. There was a horrible clanger moment of silence, just like that bit at the end of *Oranges and Lemons* when Pam used to get the chopper to chop off her head. Paige burst into floods tears. Mr Whatever-his-name-was, handed her tissue after tissue, and sat with her in silence, while she cried it out of her system.

"I can't impress on you enough, just how lucky you are to be alive… Paige, I need to ask, do you have any siblings?"

Paige blew her nose and composed herself. "I have a sister in the UK, I've no idea where. We were put in an orphanage when our parents died then I was adopted and brought here."

"I see. I'm afraid the heart condition you have may be genetic, you need to try and find her. Do you remember the name of the orphanage?"

"No, I was only seven, my sister was fourteen."

"Hmm, highly unlikely it exists anyway, you could try searching the internet? She needs to be informed. Paige, it's possible your sister could be a ticking time bomb."

***

Pam sat in the doctor's waiting room reading *Beautiful House* magazine. A toddler rocked happily on a wooden horse while his heavily pregnant mother sat gossiping on her mobile phone. A door opened, Dr. Davies appeared and called Pam's name. She followed him into the consulting room.

"How can I help you today, Mrs Jones?"

"It's probably nothing, but, well, it's my heart, it sort of flutters sometimes." Pam hesitated. "I know, it sounds silly, right?"

Dr. Davies put a stethoscope in his ears, placed it on Pam's chest and listened. "When did you first notice this?"

"About a week ago, I kept thinking it would go."

"It's a little irregular, could be due to one of several reasons, sugar, stress, allergy, worst case – a heart defect."

"A heart defect?"

Dr. Davies took his stethoscope off and smiled, reassuringly. "Don't worry, heart defects are very rare, do you have any family history of heart problems?"

"Not that I know of."

"Have you been under stress at all?"

"I've quit my job and relocated up here, the move was a bit stressful, being on my own as a single parent, and my sons have started their new school, today in fact."

"Are you starting a new job here?"

"I haven't sorted that out yet."

"What kind of work do you do?"

"I'm a bereavement counsellor."

Dr. Davies cocked his head. "Interesting, why death?"

"My parents were killed in a car accident and my husband died in a motorbike accident seven years ago. I thought by helping others it might help me, come to terms with the loss."

"How tragic, I'm sorry to hear that, Mrs Jones, and has it?"

"I think it has been somewhat cathartic, I'm not afraid of death anymore."

"Good, don't be afraid, you know how the saying goes; death is only the beginning."

"Hey, I like that, I shall hold onto that thought." Pam grinned.

"There may be some counselling work here if you're interested?

We're a close-knit community, you know." Dr. Davies smiled.

"Thank you, doctor that's really kind but I'm taking a year off while I concentrate on getting the house into shape. There's so much to do and I'm worn out."

"I'd say that explains the palpitations. Moving house is right up there at number three in the stress chart. What brings you to this neck of the woods?"

"You get a lot more for your money compared to London. My parents did the opposite, they moved *from* here *to* London, that's when we had the crash."

"In that case, welcome home, Mrs Jones. I'm going to prescribe you some beta blockers, take two with food, twice a day, that should settle it, and make an appointment to come back in ten days to see Dr. Masters."

"Dr. Masters?"

"I'm retiring the end of this week. Dr. Masters is taking over, so make sure you fix that follow up appointment."

***

Paige was in her sprawling office, staring at the computer screen. Her black and white springer spaniel plopped down beside her, occasionally scratching at her leg and whimpering. Paige took her glasses off, rubbed her weary eyes and gazed at the panoramic view of the sun setting over the sea through the bi-fold doors. "Lily, I will take you sweetheart, one more Pamela Edwards, the fiftieth one today, then I promise to stop."

***

Pam was at the sink, singing happily as she washed up the dishes in her tiny cottage kitchen in the middle of nowhere. She couldn't care less it was small, it was hers and the boys', which meant creepy Carl couldn't get his dirty mitts on it, and that was all that mattered. The boys sat on wooden crates amongst a sea of boxes heartily eating chips out of the paper, chatting excitedly about their new home plans. Suddenly, Josh jumped to his feet.

"I need the loo!"

Harry guffawed. "You always do that, every time you sit down to eat, you're such a dork."

Josh poked out his tongue, mouthed the word 'idiot' and ran out the room.

"What are we doing this weekend, Mum?" Harry asked.

***

Paige was at her desk, typing. The name *Pamela Jones nee Edwards* appeared, she clicked on it, a profile picture emerged on the screen. She stared intently at the profile picture for a whole minute. On her desk was an old black and white photo – two little girls huddled together. She picked it up, put her glasses back on and examined it closely. The older one had a distinctive mole on her upper lip. She glanced from the picture in her hand to the one on the screen. The woman had a distinctive mole on her upper lip.

"Oh my God… it *is* you." She clicked on 'send private message' and started typing.

***

The BT engineer handed Pam his empty tea mug. "All done, my love."

"Ah, great, thank you."

"Your line should be connected in about thirty days."

Pam's smile faded. "Thirty days! But I need access to the internet."

"The internet?" The engineer chuckled at Pam's naivety. "That will take even longer, sorry love, we're a bit old-fashioned here, you know."

Pam walked back into the kitchen muttering and tutting to herself, while the boys finished off their chips. She put the mug in the sink, snuck a pot of pills out of her pocket and placed them discreetly on the windowsill.

"Who was at the front door?" Harry asked.

"The engineer, reminding me how behind the times it is down here. When we'll have internet is anyone's guess, and my phone signal is rubbish here. I was hoping to find Paige. I really wanted you both to meet her."

"You can send a text if you stand on the gate and hold it in the air." said Harry.

"Can you see me standing on the gate Harry?"

Harry changed the subject. "Me and Mum are painting the house this weekend Josh, and pruning the rose bush."

"Oh what! Can I prune the rose bush?"

"Not tonight, Josephine," Harry teased.

"Not fair, why can't I do something?" Josh sulked.

"Because you're a plonker."

Josh poked his tongue out at his big brother. Harry scrunched his empty chip paper into a ball and threw it into Josh's face. Pam intervened.

"Harry, stop it! Josh, don't be silly. There's plenty to do, let's not worry about it now, we've got the whole weekend to…"

"To explore!" cried Josh, excited.

"To unpack," replied Pam, dead-pan.

"Poo," Josh grumbled.

"I'm playing, of course you can explore, darling. Somewhere underneath that undergrowth is a garden full of secrets…"

Harry had a mischievous glint in his eye, he raised his eyebrows, then winked at Josh.

"Off you go, you two, start unpacking your bedroom boxes, make your rooms nice and cosy."

"Mum, can I put my new Tupac poster up?" Harry asked.

"Of course, sweetheart." Pam smiled.

"Yes!" Harry punched the air, picked up his chip paper up and threw it in the bin. Josh copied. The pair of them scurried off.

It had been a long and tiresome first day. The boys were fast asleep. Peace at last. No more fighting and squabbling. Pam tiptoed along the hall and gently closed her bedroom door. She picked up the crumpled black and white photo and smoothed out the creases, gazing fondly at the picture of two little girls before propping it back against her bedside lamp. Something crunched underfoot. Pam winced, a tiny drop of blood trickled from her foot. She picked up the stray glass fragment and put it on the windowsill with the rest of the glass from the frame which had fallen off the wall earlier and smashed into smithereens. She carefully removed the photo inside the broken frame and climbed into bed. Holding the photo close to her heart, Pam stared at it until the photo became blurry and a tear dropped onto the handsome smiling face of Joshua Harry Jones. She wiped it away with her threadbare pink dressing gown belt.

"I miss you so much, not a day goes by I don't think about you, one day we'll be reunited, until then, night-night my angel, I love you." Pam kissed the photo, held it next to her heart, huddled into her pillow and closed her eyes.

***

Paige opened an eye. A shaft of sunlight streamed through the gap in the curtains. An alarm shrieked loudly. She reached out to hit the snooze button, knocking her tatty fluffy owl onto the floor in the process. Her one eye focused on the picture of two little girls she had placed carefully on her bedside table. Feeling a warm glow, she drifted back to sleep…

The room was bare and scrubby with a musty smell and an atmosphere much like that of a prison cell. The orphanage matron, a proper she-devil, her big fat stomach oozing through the buttons of her grey army-like uniform, squeezed herself between the two girls as they sobbed hysterically and clung to each other. She grabbed the older one by the arms, wrenched her away and pointed to the younger child.

"Take her, quickly!" she bellowed to the devastated looking couple cowering in the corner of the room.

The young woman broke down and turned to her husband. "I can't do it, Frank, this is awful."

The matron glowered at her. "There's no nice way of doing this, so the sooner you do it, the sooner it will be over, it's for the best, hurry up!"

The young man lunged forward and scooped the crying seven-year-old into his arms. The older girl, held back by matron, reached out with all her strength, just enough to reach her little sister's fingertips and give her a fluffy owl. "No matter what happens to us, Paige, wherever we are, we are sisters, we will find each other, I promise."

The girls' eyes fixated on each other as if to hold on to the moment forever. The older girl released her grip on the owl and the couple took the little girl away, screaming…

"Pam!" Paige shouted out loud, waking herself up. Eyes wide open, she stared at the ceiling.

***

Eyes wide open, Pam stared at the ceiling. She was hot and perspiring, gasping for air, her heart pounding in her chest. In the dark she fumbled for her tablets on the bedside table but knocked them onto the floor. She tried to reach but couldn't and fell back onto the bed almost paralysed. She shouted the boys' names as loud as she could but the sound that came out of her mouth was barely audible. She could feel herself getting weaker by the second. Her heartbeat became slower and slower, her breathing became shallower and shallower until… she breathed one long final breath.

***

Harry rummaged around the kitchen cupboards trying and failing to find cereal. "MU-UM! WHERE'S THE CEREAL!" he shouted, exasperated.

A happy Josh entered the kitchen. "Yay, it's the weekend! Where's Mumma?"

"I don't know, in the shower or something, I can't find where she's put the stupid cereal."

"She's not, I've just been in the bathroom."

"God sakes, go and wake her up then, see if she wants a cup of tea."

"Ooh, can I make the tea!"

"Yes, muttonhead, go and wake Mum up first."

Harry continued sifting through the cupboard while Josh bounced off up the stairs like Tigger. Where he got his energy from first thing in the morning Harry did not know.

Moments later Josh called out, "Harry! Mum won't wake up!"

"Tell her she's going to get the wet flannel treatment!" Harry shouted back, still rummaging through the cupboards. Success, finally. At last he had tracked down the elusive Coco Pops.

"Harry!" Josh yelled. "Mum's not answering me… and she's cold!"

Harry dropped the cereal packet onto the floor, Coco Pops scattered everywhere.

Harry stood in the doorway, and froze. Josh was at the foot of the bed, petrified. His mum was lying there, motionless, her mouth slightly open, her skin was white and waxy, her eyes almost closed. One arm was holding her chest, the other arm was outstretched. A pot of spilt pills and a photograph lay on the floor next to the bed. He rushed over to his mum's bedside.

"Mum? Wake up, this isn't funny, MUM?!" Harry leaned in and put his face in front of her mouth, no air came out. He placed two fingers on her neck... nothing. He shook her... nothing. He shook her and shook her... still nothing. Hands shaking, he grabbed her cold wrist and felt for a pulse... nothing. Hysteria welled up inside him. "MUM! PLEASE! WAKE UP!"

Josh had turned green and was quivering from head to toe. He backed away slowly from the end of the bed. Harry gave his mum the kiss of life, over and over, she remained unresponsive. Josh started gagging uncontrollably, he retched and ran out of the room.

Harry performed cardiac massage repeatedly, desperately, begging for her to wake up. Exhausted from trying, he stopped and examined his mother's ghostly face. No movement whatsoever. Her mouth remained slightly open, she was white as a sheet, her eyes mostly closed but for a slit. In the slit he could see her eyes were like marbles, there was no life in them. The sun shone through the bedroom window, casting an orange glow over her, she looked peaceful, almost holy. He gently took hold of her outstretched arm and tried to move it, but it was rigid. Harry's eyes brimmed with tears as he absorbed the enormity of what had happened. She had gone. He picked up the fallen photo from the bedroom floor and carefully slid it into her stiff hand. Devastated, Harry collapsed on top of his mother and howled his lungs out.

Somehow, Harry managed to put one foot in front of the other. Stiff as a plank, he walked into his brother's bedroom. Josh was on the floor, in the corner of the room, curled into a ball. His head buried firmly between his knees, his arms wrapped tightly around himself.

"Josh... buddy... I don't know how to say this... Mum's..."

Josh remained a ball. "Don't say it! Please don't say it!" he shouted into his chest, rocking back and forth.

Harry didn't feel too steady. He flopped down next to his little brother before he keeled over and fell against the radiator. He picked a piece of Blu Tack off the floor and started pulling and stretching it. "Mum's got rigor mortis… like in that *Day of the Dead* film."

Josh slowly lifted his wobbling head, his eyes pleading with his big brother. "Help me, please, Harry, help me, I don't know what to do." He started to cry.

Seeing the pain in his brother's eyes, Harry grabbed hold of him. "Don't be scared, Josh, be strong." He wrapped his arms protectively around him. Harry was trying so hard to be brave, but the tears still managed to fall out of his squeezed shut eyes. Harry huddled together with his little brother, and clung on for their dear lives.

Harry had spent far too long pacing around the house, crying and panicking, wondering what to do. Josh was still his room, quiet as a mouse. He couldn't just sit there, forever, with a mouth tasting of sick, they had to deal with this. Hands shaking, he poured his little brother a glass of water and went back up the dreaded stairs. Josh was still curled into a ball in the corner of his room. Harry bent down and handed him the drink.

"Josh, here you go…"

Josh did not respond.

"JOSH!"

Slowly he unravelled. A wobbly arm reached out and took the glass. Harry sighed and sat down on the floor next to him.

"I flushed your sick away, bud."

"Thanks."

"Josh, we have to deal with this."

"I don't want to deal with it."

"Me either, but we have to."

"I don't understand what's happened to Mum, Harry."

"Me too, I thought she'd, you know, so I counted the pills on the floor, there was only two missing, the ones she took when we were having chips, when you went to the toilet…"

***

Harry had been stuffing his face with chips. One eye on his iPhone the other on his mum, eagle-eyed Harry noticed as she snuck two tablets out of a pill pot then discreetly placed the pot back on the kitchen windowsill. She'd swallowed them quickly, resumed washing up and carried on singing. "Mum, what are they?"

"Oh, nothing much, just some pills the doctor gave me today."

"What sort of pills?"

"To calm my heartrate down, I've been rushing around a bit too much."

Worried, Harry had stopped munching, a half-eaten chip hanging from his mouth. "Heart pills?"

"No, chill pills that's all, nothing to worry about."

"Good. I don't want you to die." Harry had resumed munching his half-eaten chip. "We did first aid at school today. I had to resuscitate a dummy."

His mum had dried her hands and pulled up a crate next to him. "If anything did happen to me, not that it will, but if it did, you must never EVER tell a soul, you know that, don't you?"

Josh returned from his trip to the toilet. Upon seeing his little brother, Harry switched his attitude from worried son to sarcastic teenager. "Yes, I know, Mum, if anything ever happens to you, rah, rah, rah, the authorities will put us in an orphanage."

"And we'll never see each other again, like you and your sister," added Josh.

"Well remembered, and do you remember what I told you, Harry, when you cried when they put Dad's body in the ground?"

In a bored monotone, Harry repeated the famous sentence word for word. "It's not your dad. It's only his empty shell."

"Dad is an angel now, looking after us."

"He is, Joshy, he's a twinkling star in the sky, and I'll tell you something I tell all my clients, don't be afraid of death, we're all on the same bus, some of us get off early and some of us stay on, but we're all going to the same party, and we will all be together in the end."

"I'm not scared of death," a brazen Harry had stated.

"Me either," Josh had copied.

"Good, because there's nothing to be afraid of." Their mum had smiled lovingly at her sons. "Death is only the beginning…"

***

"Do you think we should call the doctor, Harry…Harry?"

Harry was a million miles away, staring into space. "Huh?"

"Or call an ambulance or something?"

"What's the point in that?" Harry snapped. "What are they going to do? She's dead. Don't you get it?"

Josh retreated into a ball.

"I'm sorry, Josh… I shouldn't have said that."

"No, you shouldn't! She's not dead! She got off the bus… that's all."

"Yeah… that's it… Mum got off the bus."

"Do you think we should call the police?"

"Yes, no, maybe, oh I don't know, if we do, they will put us in an orphanage, Josh…"

"And take me away…"

"And we'll be split up like Mum and her sister."

"What are we going to do, Harry?"

"There's only thing we can do. Remember what we did with Scooby the hamster?"

"What, you mean, when he died...." Josh gulped. "Harry! We can't put Mum in the ground!"

"Mum told us never EVER to tell anyone Josh, what choice do we have?"

"Mum's an angel, isn't she... what do you think she's saying to us, Harry?"

"It's not her, it's only her empty shell."

"But I don't want to bury Mum, it feels wrong."

"Can you think of a better idea?"

"She can stay in the bedroom and we can put a blanket over her." Josh sounded full of hope.

"She'll decompose, Josh."

"What does that mean?"

"Rot."

Josh grimaced and curled back into a ball.

"Look, we can survive, Mum's got money in a safe under her bed, she didn't want to put it in the bank in case Uncle Carl found out, so we can use that, then I can get a job when I'm fifteen and look after you."

Josh unravelled himself. "What if someone finds out?"

"Nobody will ever know, we'll pretend Mum's still around."

"But I'm scared, Harry, I'm really scared."

"Me too. I'm scared of us being put in an orphanage, some family will take you away, what's scarier, Josh? Burying Mum? Or never seeing each other again?"

Josh started to cry. "I don't want us to be split up! I don't want to live with another family far away!"

"I won't let that happen, I won't let anyone take you away, Joshy. I promise."

"I'm scared of that more than anything."

"Me too, and what's the one thing we're not scared of, Josh?"

"Death?"

"Then we've got no choice… we have to do it… we have to bury Mum… you in, brother?"

Harry, with his hand poised in the air, waited… slowly, Josh raised his shaking hand, they high fived then performed a wobbly special handshake.

"I'm in, brother."

CHAPTER THREE

BURNT TOAST

Harry, with his eyes squeezed shut tight, felt his way into the bedroom. He got down on all fours and wriggled under the bed. The fingers on his mother's outstretched arm hooked themselves onto the back of his jumper. He froze.

"Mum?" Pondering, for a moment there, he almost thought…

No answer. He reached behind him and felt her cold hand. He rocked back and forth. The stiff fingers remained attached. Nope – she definitely wasn't alive. Harry pushed his heartbreak to one side, like the terminator he had to be fearless, he had to do this. He took a deep breath, distorted his body until the stiff fingers unhooked themselves and wriggled out from under the bed. Harry didn't want to look, he really didn't want to… accidentally catch a glimpse of his mum's ghostly grey face. His stomach churned at the sight. He squeezed his eyes shut tight, took hold of his mum's outstretched arm and pushed it back, this time with force, cringing, as if it were about to snap. Luckily, it didn't. He quickly pulled the duvet over her then squeezed himself back under the bed and backed out with a sleeping bag in one hand, a metal safe in the other.

It was tipping down with rain as Harry and Josh dragged the heavy sleeping bag up the garden to the secret den. Harry scraped the wet mud away, then one, two, three, he removed the lid and quickly slithered into the dark hole. He pulled the sleeping bag in, it dropped with a thud, Josh recoiled. Harry reached up. In the dark, he could just about make out Josh's silhouette facing the other way. "Don't look down Josh, just let me grab hold of your hands."

Still facing the other way, trembling like a blancmange, Josh reached down into the disused cesspit. Harry grabbed hold of his shaky arms and clambered out.

Harry shovelled wet heavy mud from the ginormous earth mound into the wheelbarrow. Josh copied. Sheets of rain cascaded from the sky. It wasn't easy, slipping and sliding in the wet mud, but they kept at it, like terminators, until Josh slipped and fell against the wheelbarrow almost knocking it over.

"Clumsy fool!" shouted Harry.

Josh crumbled. "Stop it!" He threw his shovel onto the ground.

"What are you doing, Josh?"

"I can't do it, it feels wrong!"

Harry paused for a moment, shaking off the tiny droplets of rain clinging defiantly to the edges of his hair. "What do you suggest we do? Huh?" Sweating, angry, soaked through to the skin, he carried on shovelling.

"The church graveyard up the road, can't we put her there?"

Harry threw his spade into the mound like a spear. "Do you want to be put in an orphanage?! DO YOU?! This isn't easy for me either you know!"

Josh picked up his shovel. Terminator Harry picked up his, and they continued shovelling until the wheelbarrow was full to overflowing.

"It's not Mum, it's her empty shell, Josh, Mum's an angel now… with Dad, come on, help me push this thing."

With Josh's help, for what it was worth, Harry heaved the heavy wheelbarrow over to the cesspit and tipped the wet mud into the hole. Backwards and forwards they went, backwards and forwards, battling against the driving rain, soaked through to the skin, until the last bit of mud had been shovelled into the wheelbarrow.

Harry tipped the final barrow of mud into the hole and patted it down with the back of his shovel. He carefully replaced the lid, got down on his hands and knees and, using his bare hands, scraped wet sticky mud across the lid. Josh passed him a box of grass seed and he sprinkled it over the top. Aching from head to toe, Harry stood and arched his back. At last, the rain had stopped and the clouds had all but cleared. He looked up at the night sky.

"Look at the stars, Josh."

Josh looked up, his bewildered face red beneath the mud and wet, his hair and clothes saturated and caked in dirt. "This is even more of a secret place now, Harry…"

A star twinkled extra bright. "Harry! Look! Mum's a twinkling star in the sky!"

"She is, Joshy, death is only the beginning," said Harry, placing a soggy arm around his little brother's shoulders.

***

"I've found her!" Paige squealed with excitement as she lay on the bed for her post-op check.

"Seems to be healing nicely." Mr Gangulu smiled, feeling around her upper waist. "You'll be back to your old self in no time, Paige." He pulled her jumper back down.

Paige sat bolt upright. "I couldn't believe it! Now I'm thinking, damn, why didn't I do this years ago? I've sent several messages, I told her all about the gene but she hasn't answered me, it's really odd."

"Perhaps she doesn't want to be found."

"What do you mean? Why wouldn't she want me to find her?" Paige was confused.

"I've seen it happen, it can be traumatic for some people when their past life catches up, you may have to face facts, she's moved on."

"No, my sister wouldn't do that to me. I know she wouldn't."

The consultant smiled. "You've done the right thing informing her of the health risks, there's not a lot more you can do."

Paige bowed her head, disappointed.

***

A bright and crisp morning. Smartly dressed in their uniforms. The boys trundled down the lane on their way to school, just like every other normal day… except it wasn't a normal day, and Harry knew it. Josh walked beside him in total silence. They passed the graveyard, Josh stopped and looked at the headstones. Not this, again. Harry rolled his eyes.

"Josh. Come on," Harry carried on walking

"I can't!" Josh shouted.

Frustrated, Harry stopped, counted silently to five on his fingers then turned around and calmly walked back to Josh.

"Two weeks you've been stuck in that bedroom, apart from sneaking out to stare at the stupid graveyard, people will get suspicious, the authorities will come round and…"

"I know! You keep saying. They'll put us in an orphanage."

"Look Josh, I know this is hard, but please, hang in there, buddy, it's the summer holidays in a few weeks, things will be better, I promise."

Josh rubbed his teary eyes. Harry put an arm around his shoulder and slowly they continued their journey to school.

Harry paced around in the lounge, his eyes glued to his iPhone, that way he didn't have to deal with how sparse and un-homely the place was. Two sofas were awkwardly positioned in front of the television. There were no curtains, no ornaments, only a bucket of wood next to the fire and two plates covered in congealed baked bean juice left to rot on the floor. Harry tore his eyes away from the screen to look out of the window. He shook his head in exasperation. There was Josh, sitting cross-legged, on top of the secret den, snivelling and picking the newly grown grass.

"Twit," Harry said to himself. And stormed outside.

"Josh! Get off! How many times have I told you! And where were you when the bell went? I waited for you at the school gate for ages!" He grabbed Josh and yanked him roughly off the grass patch. "Don't keep sitting here Josh you will draw attention to us."

Josh glared daggers at him. "I HATE YOU!" he screamed at the top of his lungs. "I WANT TO GO HOME!" He ran off and left Harry standing there, like a plum.

Harry knew what he meant, Josh wanted to go back to their old house, to their old life, when they still had their mum, if only…

***

The beds had been dismantled ready for the move first thing in the morning. Harry had climbed into his sleeping bag on the mattress next to his little brother. Their mum had kissed them both goodnight.

"Soon we'll have our own little cottage far away and nobody can take it from us. I've got quite a bit of money left so I'm going to take time out and have some fun with you guys. It'll be a fresh start for all of us."

Josh had punched the air, excited. "A fresh start! Yay! Harry, it'll be really good, I can't wait! Mum's buying us a moving in present she said, I'm getting a PlayStation."

Intrigued, Harry had smiled at that. "Really?"

"Really, you are such good boys, when you're not fighting."

"What are you going to get me Mum?"

"I'll tell you in the morning. Now, get some sleep, we've got a big day ahead of us. It's going to be an adventure, boys, the biggest one yet…"

Harry didn't want to do it, he really didn't, but he had to. Dragging a black bin bag behind him, he took a deep breath, swallowed hard, and tentatively pushed open the door to his mum's empty bedroom. His mind flashbacked to their last night…

"Is that you, Harry?"

His mum had said as he creaked open the bedroom door. She was on her knees amongst a sea of empty boxes in her threadbare pink dressing gown. It had seen better days but Harry knew better than to mention it. He made a joke about it once and sorely regretted it. His mum had burst into tears and told him she couldn't bear to part with it, being her last ever anniversary present from his dad.

"You okay, Mum?" Harry had gotten down onto his knees beside her.

"I'm trying to find a couple of things…" she said, rooting through the box marked 'special' in big black marker pen. "Struggling to sleep, huh?"

Harry had nodded.

"I thought you might, first night, new school, new house," she said, still rummaging. "You can help me if you like… ah, here we go."

His mum had pulled out a crumpled old black and white photo of her and Paige. She smoothed out the creases and carefully propped it up against her bedside lamp. Harry had continued foraging through the box. "Is this the other thing by any chance?" Harry handed his mum her cherished wedding photo in a mirrored silver frame.

"Aw, thank you, Harry…" Her face smiled, but he could see the sadness in her eyes. He watched as she positioned it ever so carefully on a picture hook on the wall above her bed. "There we go." She turned to face Harry, there was a loud bang.

"Mum!" Harry shouted, but he was too late. The photo had fallen down, bounced off the bed and smashed into smithereens.

"Oh no, seven years bad luck!" she'd cried in despair, carefully picking up the tiny pieces of broken glass.

Harry had spotted the hole in the wall where the picture hook had fallen off, taking a big chunk of plaster with it.

"What idiot put that hook on the wall?"

"This idiot," said his mum.

The bang must have woken Josh, he walked into the room rubbing his tired eyes. "Mum's not an idiot," said sleepy Josh.

"I didn't say Mum was an idiot, big ears, did I? I thought it was the people before, idiot."

"Boys! Please, this isn't helping."

"I've got an idea." Harry disappeared and returned holding a silver framed picture of his idol, Tupac. "You can have this frame if you want, Mum."

"Oh what! Can I have the picture of Tupac then?" said Josh, suddenly wide awake.

"No, you can't. I'll get you a picture of Tinky Winky," said Harry, humming the theme tune and performing the Teletubby dance.

Josh had pulled a face, folded his arms across his chest and sulked. "Meanie."

"Why do you want my picture of Tupac? You don't even like him."

"He wants to be like you, that's why, haven't you worked it out yet, you're his idol, Harry…"

Harry's irritation had turned to pride as he contemplated the notion of being someone's idol.

"Don't worry, boys, I'm going to get a new frame, back to bed now, it's late." His mum had said. She placed the smashed frame and handful of broken glass on the windowsill. "There, all sorted." She held the photo close to her heart. "Your father can come to bed with me."

Harry had handed the framed Tupac picture to Josh. "Have it, if you want."

Josh's face had lit up. "No way! Thanks, Harry!"

"You're a chip off the old daddy block, Harry, your father would be so proud…" Their mum had kissed them both on the head. "Goodnight, my loves, sleep tight, busy weekend, pruning and painting ahead."

"Good night, Mum." They had both said.

"I love you both to the stars and back, you know…" she said.

And they were the last words she ever said…

Harry swept the broken glass fragments off the windowsill into the bin bag. He walked over to the bedside locker and picked up his mother's lipstick, he opened it and closed it – opened it and closed it, then sniffed it. The sweet smell of her lips when she used to kiss him goodnight was painfully fresh in his mind. He placed the lipstick ever so carefully back on the bedside table then left the empty bedroom, exactly as it was, like a holy shrine.

***

So much for summer, it was a cold, windy, grey day. Josh had managed to sneak out of school before Harry so he could walk home alone and, like he always did, stop and stare at the headstones without Harry moaning at him. For some strange reason he felt drawn to the graveyard. Up ahead, Josh noticed those two nasty lads ambling up the lane toward him. Oh no, not this again. He glanced over his shoulder, no sign of Harry, in fact there wasn't a body in sight, apart from those buried underneath the headstones. He pulled his hood up, tucked his hands deep into his pockets, hoping he had made himself somehow invisible. The two boys got closer and closer until… Josh tried to walk past but every which way, they blocked his path.

"Look who it isn't. London boy," sneered the first one.

"Moody pants," sniggered the second one.

The bullies passed either side of Josh and bashed into him, purposefully knocking his school bag to the ground. His keys, books and pens spewed out; the horrible lads trampled over his books, kicking his stuff, taunting him and laughing. They ran off leaving Josh on all fours gathering his bits together. Josh looked over at the graveyard. A shaft of heavenly light cascaded down, lighting up the headstones. For a split second there he could have sworn he saw his mum, sitting on the church step. He blinked and she was gone.

***

Harry and Holley stopped outside the front gate. Harry watched as Josh wiped the grass off his backside and quickly sat on the front doorstep, as if he had been sitting there the whole time, like nobody would know, the slimy pilchard.

"Why doesn't your brother walk home with us anymore?" Holley asked.

"I don't know, I can't believe he dropped his keys, he's being such a numpty about everything lately."

Harry walked through the gate, Holley lingered. "Harry, I was wondering, I mean, maybe we could do that History homework together."

Harry closed the gate behind himself. "I can't. I've got to do tea for Josh and, um, some other stuff, sorry."

Holley blushed. "It was just a thought. It must be difficult with your mum ill all the time, never mind, see you later."

Harry cursed silently and kicked himself. He so badly wanted to say yes, but he couldn't. He watched her walk away and turned his annoyance in the direction of his stupid little brother. "Where are your keys?"

Josh shrugged his shoulders. Harry dangled a set of keys in his face then threw them into his lap. "Jerk. I found them down the lane. I know you've been sitting there again."

Josh frowned. "I haven't!"

"Whatever!" Harry stepped over Josh and let himself in the front door.

So what if the kitchen side was a complete mess, brimming with dirty cups, plates and bowls and the rubbish bin overflowing. To be fair, Harry had made an effort. He had hung curtains on the poles in the lounge and put the kitchen table together so they had somewhere to sit and eat. It was a bit rickety but a step up from sitting on the floor. It was hard work this playing mum lark. Harry watched as Josh tutted and struggled with his homework.

He put some bread in the toaster, grabbed a pen and paper out of his school bag and joined his brother at the wobbly table.

"What are you doing?" Josh asked.

"Your teacher wanted a note you said, about why you've had two weeks off." Harry folded the note, handed it to Josh and went back to his cooking chores.

"It's signed from Mum?" Josh looked horrified.

"Of course it is, stupid, don't look at it, just give it to your teacher in the morning," said Harry, opening a tin of macaroni cheese.

"Not again, boring." Josh frowned. "We had that yesterday."

Harry snapped. "No, we didn't, we had beans, shut up and get on with your homework."

"We had it the day before then! I don't want it! I'm fed up with stuff on burnt toast! Every day we have burnt toast! And I don't understand this stupid homework! You never help me! Mum used to help me! And she made me fish fingers!"

Josh threw his pen down, elbowed his schoolbook off the table and stormed off. Smoke poured out of the toaster. Harry watched as two miserable slices of burnt toast popped up. What was the point of life?

***

"Life is for living." Ginger smiled and raised her coffee cup.

How right was she, and how blessed was Paige, not only to be alive, but to be a lady of leisure. Golden sunlight beamed into her luxurious sitting room, reflecting onto her expensive white leather sofas. Since her life saving op, Paige had a renewed appreciation for everything.

"Come on. Let's breathe some sea air." She opened the bi-fold doors and stepped onto the wooden veranda which had steps down to her very own private white sandy beach.

Although from very different backgrounds, she shared a lot in common with her best friend, the flamboyant but loveable Ginger. One of those things being money. Ginger was also a lady of leisure, only she didn't win a colossal sum of money like Paige had, she was born into wealth thanks to her father's property empire on the Gold Coast. The wonder of peroxide and plastic surgery allowed her to look a lot younger than her forty years. Now that – was something they didn't have in common.

Paige lifted her t-shirt, showing off her neat pink scar extending from beneath her belly button all the way up to her ribcage. Ginger inhaled a sharp intake of breath and gawped.

"Amazing! They made more mess when I had that mini facelift. Do you remember those awful bruises on my face?"

Paige giggled at the memory. "Do I remember? I thought you'd gone missing."

"I know, I had to go into hiding. It's not the sort of hideous thing you want people to see."

"And when you did surface, you wore those awful big dark glasses for weeks."

"Now you're just being cruel… hey, I've been meaning to ask, has your sister in the UK responded yet?"

"No, she hasn't." Paige sighed. "I sent three messages and I still haven't heard. It's been over a month now, the doc thinks she doesn't want to know."

"What do you think?"

"I have a nasty gut feeling something's happened to her."

CHAPTER FOUR

SEVEN YEARS BAD LUCK

Harry poked his head around the bedroom door, no sign of Josh. He raced downstairs into the lounge, no sign of Josh. He glanced around the room, despondent. Somehow, it had become increasingly untidy. The mess-fairies must have paid them a visit. Empty Coke cans, pizza boxes, pot noodles, lay scattered amongst a sea of dirty clothes and junk. Cobwebs swung from the ceiling, the place was in dire need of a good hoover and dust. Harry stared through the window at the newly grown grass patch, no sign of Josh. He looked at his watch, paced around the grotty lounge for a bit, then peered through the window again, still no sign of Josh. Harry flopped onto the sofa pointed the remote at the TV and started aimlessly channel flicking, hoping to find a film he could immerse himself in, and forget all about the pain in the bum that was his little brother. *Seven Years in Tibet* caught his eye. Seven years bad luck more like – the words came back to haunt him. His mum had said that the night she died.

***

"Don't listen to that nasty gut feeling, I'm sure she's okay," encouraged Ginger.

"So why hasn't she responded?"

"Maybe she's busy."

"Or, the doc's right and I'm wrong, she doesn't want to know."

"I think this Pam business is eating you away, I mean, you've always been slender, but you're looking way too thin."

"Nothing to do with the fact I've just had a major life-saving op." Paige raised her eyebrows

"Oh, darl, you've been through so much, it's not fair she should at least tell you, stop you worrying and wondering forever, why not send one more message?"

"And say what?"

"I don't know, maybe keep it simple this time, make it easy for her."

"Maybe…" said Paige, collating the empty coffee cups and pondering for a moment. Maybe not, she concluded and went back inside the house.

***

Harry leant over the gate, he looked up the lane, no sign of Josh. He looked down the lane, no sign of Josh. He took his iPhone out of his pocket and started texting then climbed on top of the gate, he had one bar of signal if he held his phone in the air. He waited. Twenty fingernail-biting minutes later, Holley appeared, puffing and panting.

"Sorry, my dad wouldn't let me out until I'd finished my homework. What's wrong, Harry?"

"My brother. I think he's run away." Harry jumped down from the gate.

"Why would he?"

"My mum…"

"What's wrong with your mum now?"

"Oh, you know, the usual, tired of cooking, cleaning and that, hard work, isn't it, playing mum… I mean, being a mum, and Josh not doing as he's told."

"Aw, poor Josh, sounds like he's trying to let go of your mum's apron strings."

"What do you mean?" asked Harry, feeling extremely paranoid.

"You know, growing up, when my mum left us, I had to grow up quick."

"My mum hasn't left us," Harry snapped.

"I didn't mean it like that." Holley blushed. "I mean she's always ill or works a lot, that's all."

Relief washed over Harry. "Oh right, yeah."

"Have you told your mum?"

"NO… I mean no, not yet, I don't want to worry her."

"Good idea. Okay. Let's think about this. Where might he go?"

"Hmm." Harry looked thoughtful for a moment. "I think I might know."

Not the nicest of places to hang out, but he of all people, knew why. By now it was dusk as Harry climbed over the turnstile into the eerie graveyard. He shuddered at the shimmering mist lingering above the ground, weaving its way through the graves and adding perfectly to the spookiness of it.

"Why would he want to come here?" asked Holley as she climbed over the turnstile.

Harry sighed. "Don't ask."

"It's so creepy."

"He's obsessed with the place."

"I feel like Michael Jackson's going to appear any minute."

Harry spun around like a ghoul and pulled the *Thriller* pose. Holley jumped back and smacked him on the arm. "Fool."

Harry managed a small laugh. He hadn't done that in a while.

The teenagers crept around the murky headstones until they reached the path leading to the church. They got closer and closer…

"There he is!" Holley pointed through the fog.

Harry squinted through the dusky mist. He could just about make out a silhouette sat on the cold step, leaning against the grey church building, gazing up at the stars in the night sky.

"Josh!" Harry called out, he sprinted up the path with Holley.

"There you are…" said Harry, out of breath. "What are you doing?"

Josh curled himself into a ball. "Go away," he mumbled into his chest.

"Come on, buddy," pleaded Harry.

Josh lifted his head. "You're not my buddy though! Are you?" he shouted through his tears.

Ouch, that hurt, Harry was offended. He raised his hands in surrender. "Whoa, relax Max."

Josh responded by curling back into a ball.

"Hey, Josh? What's up?" caring Holley asked.

Harry stomped off in a mood. Josh remained a ball. "He doesn't care about me…" He lifted his head and shouted at the top of his voice. "HE ONLY CARES ABOUT HIMSELF!"

Harry stopped in his tracks and turned around. His face red and fuming. Snorting like a bull, he charged ready to fight.

"That's not true, he's worried about you, he told me about your mum."

Josh gawped at Holley. "You mean... you know?"

Harry grabbed hold of Josh by the scruff off the neck. They tussled around on the ground, shouting, fists flying.

"Stop it, please! Harry!" Holley cried.

Harry carried on fighting, unable to stop. Holley muscled in and tried to pull him off Josh. A fist flew up and knocked her backwards. Harry heard a thump as she fell onto the ground. He released his grip on his little brother.

"Now look what you've done!" He glared at Josh, slumped against the church wall, his hair a total mess, his shirt ripped from top to bottom.

"It wasn't him, it was you actually." Holley grinned.

"Oh... cripes, sorry." Gutted, Harry helped her up off the floor.

Holley brushed the dirt off her jeans. "I'm fine, honest, they needed a wash anyway."

Josh pulled a face at him. It was an awkward moment – until Holley burst into a giggle fit. The awkward ice was broken. Dishevelled, Harry plonked himself down next to Josh.

"You didn't have to tell her," loud-mouthed Josh, whispered in his ear.

"It's okay, Josh." said Holley, adopting a motherly manner and snuggling up next to Harry on the cold step. "I went through the same thing with my mum when I was younger."

"What... you... buried her?"

"Her ring! He means..." Harry intervened, raising his eyebrows at Josh and pinching his leg at the same time. He turned to face Holley. "I told him you, um, buried your mum's ring because you were angry, didn't you?" Harry winked at her profusely.

"Oh, the ring! Yeah, I did. Nice gold one it was, with lots of little diamonds, I was so angry I got hold of it and dug a big hole in the garden and…"

"Anyway," Harry interrupted. "Why don't we forget all this rubbish, come home, hey Josh?"

Harry felt a pang of remorse, but not quite enough to justify the special handshake. He was old enough to know better, his mum always said, he was also old enough to know his stubborn little brother would never back down. Harry, the bigger man, held out his hand, Josh reluctantly pulled himself up.

"I'm sorry, bud, it's okay to be upset. I do understand," said Harry. "But you won't find what you're looking for here."

"Not unless you were hoping to see a ghost," Holley added.

The stubborn one was tucked up in his cosy bed gazing at the glow in the dark stars Harry had stuck on the ceiling for him as a peace offering. Harry, was next to him in his makeshift bed, a mattress and a sleeping bag, gazing at the real stars. *I love you to the stars and back, you know*, were the last words his mum had said. A star twinkled extra bright and a tear slid from the corner of his eye.

"Sorry about the macaroni…" said Josh.

"I thought you hated me…" Harry got up, drew the lopsided red curtains and crawled back into his makeshift bed. "Mum would have been forty tomorrow."

"At least she didn't get to be old," Josh replied, obviously trying to be helpful.

"That's when life begins for grown-ups, Mum told me, didn't for her though, did it." Harry sniffed and wiped the corner of his eye.

"It's okay to be upset, Harry, that's what you said to me."

"I've got something in my eye that's all."

"I miss Mum's cooking sometimes. I won't sit there anymore,

Harry. You did the right thing, Harry, I mean we did... we did the right thing."

Harry reached up and turned the diplodocus lamp off. "Goodnight, Josh."

Josh whispered in the dark. "Hey, Harry, remember the Blu Tack fight?"

"Yeah," Sniffed Harry. "Mum's last night..."

The boys had been grappling with each other, rolling around on Josh's bedroom floor.

"Give it back, you thieving pig!" Harry shouted.

"Get off me! It's not yours, it's mine!" screamed Josh.

"BOYS! STOP IT! PLEASE!" a voice bellowed over the top of them.

Their mum had bounded into the bedroom but the boys continued grappling and paid no attention to her distressed plea. She dived between them and wrenched them apart. Harry's nose was slightly bleeding, Josh was crying. "What in God's name is going on in here?"

"He started it!" Harry yelled.

"No, you started it!" Josh retaliated.

"He punched me in the face, the little..." Harry dabbed his bloody nose with his finger.

"You ripped my Tupac poster off the wall, that's why!"

"Yeah because you took my poster off the wall! And you stole my Blu Tack!"

"I didn't!" Josh started to cry.

Harry had got so angry he pulled back a fist and lunged toward Josh who hid behind their mum, the coward. She'd grabbed Harry just in time to stop him landing a punch on his little brother.

"Stop it, Harry! You're old enough to know better!"

"He's a liar! And a scrounging little scumbag! You always get away with it, Mummy's boy."

"I hate you!" Josh screamed through his tears, attempting to kick Harry while hiding behind the safety of his mother's legs.

Their mum had finally caved in. "So you want to hurt each other, do you? Let me tell you there are plenty of people in this world that will try to hurt you, that's why brothers and sisters should look after each other! You don't know how lucky you are…" her voice wavered.

Josh had flopped onto his bed, clutching his torn Arnold Schwarzenegger poster and sobbed into his pillow. Harry had marched out of the room slamming the door behind him, for effect.

"Right, you…" Harry had overheard his mum say. He'd pinned his ear to the door and eavesdropped. He couldn't wait to hear Josh get the roasting he deserved.

"Shall we have a hug, Josh?"

"No."

A hug? The crybaby deserved a roasting not a hug. Spoiled brat, he always got away with it.

"Alright, I'll go and see Harry, he'll give me a hug."

Harry had unpinned his ear from the door and speed-tiptoed away but a pair of hands had grabbed him from behind and shoulder marched him back into the bedroom.

"You two, we're going to sort this out! Right here, right now!"

Harry sighed at the memory. What he would give to feel those hands on his shoulders right now.

Their mum had taken a tissue from her pocket and dried Josh's eyes.

"No more tears, come on."

"It's... not... fair... he... ripped... my... poster... down," Josh snivelled.

"Because you stole my Blu Tack!" Harry retaliated.

"I DIDN'T!" Josh bawled at the top of his lungs.

"He's lying!" Harry had turned to his mum for support and she'd winked at him.

"Josh, it's written in your eyes, that's why you can't face me, look at me, please…"

Josh slowly lifted his face, squinting his eyes to hide his lies. Harry had shaken his head in disbelief while his mum stifled a smile at his little brother's pathetically unfunny attempt to conceal the truth.

"I won't tell you off for telling the truth, you know that. I'm going to ask you one more time, did you take his Blu Tack?"

Josh looked down at the floor and nodded a microscopic nod.

"Why did you take it?"

"I wanted to put my poster up," he mumbled.

"So, you took his poster down, then took his Blu Tack so you could put yours up, and when he got angry, you punched him in the face?"

Eyes to the floor, Josh nodded again, a teeny weeny, nod.

"Do you think that's fair? Do you want your brother to think you are a thief and a liar?"

"No!"

"Josh, Uncle Carl told lies, it caused so much trouble between your dad and his family, he rode off on his motorbike really angry, he took the bend too fast and…"

Josh had peeped through his lie-hiding squinty-eyes. Harry knew he was starting to feel bad, and he was too. They both hated it when she got upset about – you know what.

"Josh, I want you to be a man, and tell the truth, can you do that?"

Josh had nodded, a big bold nod.

"Good boy." She turned to Harry. "Josh has got something to say to you, haven't you, Josh?"

Josh had hung his head in shame. "I'm sorry I punched you, Harry."

Harry had felt a glow of satisfaction discovering Josh was a chip off the old daddy block after all, just like him. Their dad was man enough to apologise to his brother when he punched him, but he deserved it, unlike Harry. His mum had told him the story of how horrible ugly little man, Uncle Carl, lied through his spiteful teeth and manipulated the whole family against her. His dad went round there to have it out with them once and for all. That was the night he rode off angry, and that was the last time Harry, and his poor mum, ever saw him.

"Anything else you want to say, Josh?" Their mum had asked.

Josh lifted his head. Tears had welled up in his eyes, he collapsed into a blubbering fit. "I'm sorry, Harry!" he confessed, "I don't know why I did it! I just wanted to put my poster up!"

"All you had to do was ask." Harry was puzzled. "I've got a whole pack in my drawer."

His mum had laughed heartily at that…

"Goodnight, Harry," Josh whispered in the dark, jolting Harry back to the harsh reality of the now, and a life with no mum.

"You don't hate me then?" Harry asked.

"No, I don't hate you. I hate those two lads."

Harry reached up and turned the diplodocus lamp back on. "What two lads?"

CHAPTER FIVE

THE WOMAN AT THE WINDOW

The end of school bell screeched, everyone cheered. Harry packed his books away, he couldn't wait to get out of there. Miss Allen banged her fist on the desk like a gavel to get everyone's attention. Hiding behind the safety of his desk lid, Harry spied over the top at his young teacher. She removed her teacher shoes and squidged her feet into a pair of trainers.

"Have a good weekend, guys…" she shouted above the din.

Harry closed his desk lid, he had gotten away with it. Good old ditzy Miss Allen, and if it wasn't for that Nanny McPhee front tooth, she'd be rather fit too.

"Oh, and Harry Jones, I still haven't heard from your mum about parents evening…"

Harry, lifted his desk lid and carried on putting his imaginary books away.

"Hello? Earth calling Harry?"

The whole class laughed.

"Yes, Miss?" Harry pretended to be startled.

"Have you heard anything I've said?" she asked, tying her blonde hair into a scrunchy.

"Parents evening, Miss."

"I've got one slot at 7.15pm. I'll book your mother in for then," she said, jogging on the spot.

Harry gulped nervously.

Holley was waiting for him by the school gate as usual. The same old twice daily routine, to and from boring school. Less boring today because Harry had his partner in crime back, and the dynamic trio were on a mission.

In the distance Harry saw two lads approaching. It had to be them, surely, the way they were strutting, all Jack-the-lad, and they were older than Josh by the look of it, the cheeky beggars.

"It's them, Harry. The ones that ripped my English book," whispered Josh.

"I figured, remember what I told you buddy. Ready?"

"Ready."

Harry, with Holley in tow, diverted off in the direction of the graveyard. Holley gave Josh an exaggerated wave. Honestly, girls, talk about make it obvious. Making sure the lads didn't notice he grabbed Holley's arm, darted behind a tree and kept a watchful eye on his brother.

The boys approached and barged either side of Josh but he stood firm. He shot a questioning glance to Harry peeping out from behind the tree. Harry gave him the signal and before he could blink Josh had punched the first one in the face and kicked the second one hard between the legs… the lads groaned and fell to the floor.

Harry and Holley came running out from behind the tree. Harry pointed and fake laughed at the two wimps writhing around on the tarmac. Then, like the terminator, he stopped mid-laugh, deepened his voice and gave them his best evil stare.

"That's a warning, touch him again and you'll end up in there." He pointed at the graveyard.

The two lads scrambled to their feet and ran away as fast as their fat little legs could carry them. Mission accomplished.

"Thanks, Harry." Josh beamed.

"You pack a good punch, Josh." Harry's mind flashed back to the Blu Tack fight. "I should know," he winked.

"You're the best, Harry!" Josh raised his hand and gave him a high five.

Harry's mother's words echoed in his head...

He wants to be like you, that's why, haven't you worked that out yet, you're his idol, Harry.

"From now on things are going to change," said Harry, firmly.

Day one – operation housework. Harry scrubbed bird poo off the window and peered through the glass. Josh had de-cluttered the lounge, plumped the cushions, and straightened the rug. Next, Harry cleared the kitchen bombsite. Heaving, he scraped furry mold-covered food off plates into a black sack. Used tins, cereal packets, banana skins, rotting cheese, empty crisp packets, the whole lot, went straight in the bin. After that he tackled the washing up. Every piece of cutlery had been used. He balanced the last teaspoon precariously on the overflowing draining board, like a game of Ker-Plunk. Time for the inspection.

Josh had done well, he had de-cobwebbed and hoovered the whole house, wood lice and dead flies, excluding of course, the no-go area, the shrine that was their mum's bedroom. Mighty pleased with their joint effort, Harry nodded approvingly as he wandered around. Last inspection stop – the lounge.

"Wow, Josh, looking good."

"Not easy being a mum, is it?" sweaty Josh replied, finishing off the dusting and polishing.

"Nope, and we haven't even started yet."

Day two – operation housework. Covered head to toe in magnolia eggshell, Harry climbed down the shaky ladder and plonked himself on the grass next to his paint-stained accomplice.

"What do you reckon, Josh?" said Harry, admiring the freshly painted cottage.

"I reckon Mum would love it."

"Yeah she hated it grey."

The sun was going down and his forearms were smothered in tiny thorn cuts but Harry kept at it until he had pruned the final branch on the bedraggled rose bushes. Josh picked up the remains of the garden waste and heaved it in the wheelbarrow. Aching all over, Harry stood back and admired the neat and tidy garden.

"Good work, bro." He ruffled his little brother's hair affectionately.

And off Josh went with his last barrowful, proud as punch. Harry gazed longingly at the beautiful pink roses starting to bud. His mum would have loved those…

Harry's mind wandered back to moving day. He had waded into the kitchen through a sea of boxes, his mum was looking out of the window, waiting for the removal men.

"Mum… I was just wondering…"

"Where are they?" she tutted. "They should have been here fifteen minutes ago. Sorry, Harry, what were you wondering?"

In the kerfuffle of moving she had obviously forgotten the conversation they'd had the night before, about Josh getting a PlayStation and Harry's moving in present. He had been dying to ask, but thought better of it.

"What's the new house like?" he had asked, instead.

"Grey…" she'd pulled a face at that. "I've got to dispose of a ginormous mound of earth somehow, they dug it out for the patio then left it there, honestly…"

Then she had turned around with a big smile on her face and said, "Or, were you *really* wondering about this…" and handed him his moving in present.

"Oh my! No way! An iPhone!" Harry was taken aback. He opened the box and turned it on. "Thanks, Mum!" he beamed, fiddling excitedly with his new toy and setting his message tone to a squelchy fart sound. She had laughed at that.

"Just remember the real world Harry, that's all I ask."

"I will. I promise."

"You'd better. There's so much to do the other end. I've got to prune the overgrown roses, I can't wait to see those beautiful pink rose buds in full bloom…"

"Can I prune the roses?"

"Then I'll paint the house, after all it's called Magnolia Cottage, not Grey Cottage."

"Can I paint the house… please, Mum?"

"Don't be daft, you don't know how."

"Oh yeah?" Harry had tapped the screen on his iPhone and spoken into it loudly and clearly; "Siri, how do I prune a rose?" The phone beeped then answered in a cheesy, American, robot voice. *Looking up – how to – prune a rose.*

"At least it's capable of more than farting." His mum had chuckled.

Harry had tapped the screen and asked the phone again; "Siri, how do I paint a house?" The phone beeped. *I cannot find – how to – paint a mouse.*

The pair of them had burst into laughter… it was the last time they had laughed together…

Harry reached out and touched the budding pink rose, his eyes filled with tears and he fell against the wall, slithered down it, and collapsed into a blubbering broken heap.

***

The sun was beating down as Paige strolled along the beach, arm in arm with her friend Ginger. How beautiful the ocean was, how soft the white sand was beneath her bare feet. She was lost in the peace and tranquility of the moment, until the flamboyant one had to spoil it.

"Did you get a response from the latest message?"

"How soft is this sand?" Paige drew a heart with her foot.

"You haven't sent it, have you?"

"What's the point?" Paige kicked sand over the heart and spoiled it. "I can't do anything about it?" she sulked.

"Oh, I see… I get what this is about. Who said anything about getting on a plane? It's only a message, P."

"G, I'm banging my head on a wall, I feel like a stalker, I give up…" Paige picked up a piece of driftwood and launched it into the sea for Lily.

The dog scampered off, leaping about playfully in the rising crests of the waves as they crashed against the shoreline. Paige ran off to join her fun-loving companion.

"Life is for living!" she shouted, throwing her arms in the air and splashing her feet around in the warm sea. She had taken her life so much for granted until now, and now – was all that mattered, not the ghosts of the past.

***

Harry and Josh walked down the garden path, laden with bags of food shopping. Harry gaped in admiration. Magnolia Cottage gleamed in the glorious sunshine. The garden was neat and tidy. The beautiful pink roses were in full bloom.

"I'm so proud of you, Harry," he heard his mum say in his head, and it gave him a glow. Better times were around the corner. Just a couple more days before the summer holidays, and they couldn't come quick enough. Harry grabbed a letter out of the post box with his teeth. Josh followed him into the house.

"No way! Josh, the internet's on!"

"No way!"

"I'll have to check it when I get back. I'm going to cook some proper food before I go out."

Harry emptied the contents of his carrier bags onto the kitchen table, five tins of soup, five tins of beans and five tins of macaroni. Lastly, like a magician pulling a rabbit out of a hat, he produced a box of fish fingers.

Josh's face lit up. "Yummy! My favourite!"

Harry ruffled his little brother's hair and watched him empty the contents of his bags onto the kitchen table. A loaf of bread, Jaffa Cakes, Wagon Wheels, Club biscuits, Jammy Dodgers, chocolate chip cookies, popcorn and a humungous bag of jelly sweets.

"Damn it, Josh, we forgot toilet rolls…"

"And toothpaste… Harry where are you going tonight?"

"Parents evening. I told you."

"Can I come?"

"No, I need you to stay here."

"Why can't I come?"

"Because I have a plan, Stan..." Harry winked.

Bracing himself, Harry opened the front door. There was Holley, with her six foot something ridiculous Dad, towering over her. He understood now, why her mate Zara nicknamed him Lurch, such an unfortunate surname – Addams.

"Mum can't make it, she's um... not well." Harry stepped outside. "Bye, Mum!" he called out. "I'll let you know what they say!"

"Okay, my love – okay, my love – okay, my love," a distant female voice cried.

"Shame." Lurch eyeballed him curiously. "I was hoping to meet your elusive mother."

Harry cringed and rapidly closed the door. That crackly old video of his mum must have got stuck in a loop. He envisioned Josh in a pickle, trying to turn it off and failing because he was pointing the remote at the TV the wrong way round, like he always did, the pilchard.

It wasn't easy keeping up this charade. It was tricky being grilled by Lurch the whole way there, then being quizzed by all the teachers about why his mum was always ill. Now he had to face the prospect of a further interrogation – all the way home. Unless, perhaps, he were to phone his mum and just so happen to speak to her about parents evening – all the way home.

At last, the ordeal that was parents evening was over. Harry had pulled it off. They said their goodbyes at the gate. Harry hurried down the path.

"There's something very odd about that family," he heard Lurch say as he closed the door.

Harry leapt up the stairs two at a time and into the bedroom.

Josh was ready and waiting, in his mum's long brown wig, Gucci sunglasses and a black dress. They rushed over to the window and waved. Holley waved back. Lurch slowly raised his hand and waved it like a wimpy white flag, the loser. Harry smiled through gritted teeth and quickly drew the curtains.

Josh stepped down from the crate and removed the wig and sunglasses. Harry helped him unzip the black dress, clumps of tissue fell out onto the floor. Harry stifled a giggle.

"I'm not gay." Josh frowned.

Harry sat on his lumpy bumpy mattress browsing the laptop while Josh was in his cosy bed playing Terminator on the PlayStation. Something weird caught Harry's eye. He clicked on *new message* and read aloud;

"Hello, Pam, it's Paige, I can't believe I found you, I have something important to tell you..."

Josh threw his controller on the floor. "No way! Mum's long-lost sister!" He jumped down and ogled the screen. Harry swallowed hard and gawped at him.

***

Sleepy Paige was still in her dressing gown, since the op she had found it hard to get going in the morning. She ambled into the office and turned on the computer. She heard the computer 'ping' and was about to look but Lily pawed her leg.

"You want a biscuit? Two minutes, Lil."

She pulled up her chair, sat at her desk and was about to look at the screen but her attention was thwarted by the dog pawing her leg, again. "Biscuit more important huh? Alright then, shame you don't know how to make coffee." She got up and made her way into the kitchen.

***

Harry stared avidly at the computer and continued reading

aloud;

"After a routine op the surgeon discovered I had a life-threatening heart condition, Pam your life may be in danger as it's hereditary…"

"What does hairy de teary mean?" asked Josh.

"It means… Mum had something wrong with her heart."

"Is that why she died?"

"Must be, look at the date Josh, these messages were sent the day we moved, if only it had been the day before, Mum would have seen them… she might still be here."

"What are we going to do, Harry?"

"Ignore her, looks like she's given up, I better get offline quick, if she logs on she'll see PAM IS ONLINE in great big letters!"

***

Paige walked back into the office, carrying a cup of coffee and a dog biscuit. Yawning, she placed her coffee on the desk and spilt some in the process. "Damn." Taking a tissue out of her pocket, she wiped the spill.

***

Harry was clicking buttons frantically trying to get offline.

"Hurry up, Harry!"

"I'm trying! Poxy thing! It's crashed, the mouse isn't working!"

Paige threw the coffee drenched tissue in the waste paper bin and sat at her desk. Her attention was on Lily, not the screen. She held the biscuit in the air. "What do you say, girl?"

"Cracked it!" Harry exclaimed. "I've found the 'force-quit' key."

Lily barked ever so quietly. "Good girl, there you go." Paige handed her the biscuit and gently stroked her loveable hound.

ARE YOU SURE YOU WANT TO FORCE QUIT? PRESS CTRL. Harry tutted at the screen. "Yes, you stupid heap!"

"Quick, Harry! Press control!"

Harry's frenzied fingers twiddled with the keyboard searching for the CTRL key. "I'm trying Josh, I'm trying!"

Paige gazed lovingly at Lily. The dog finished chewing the biscuit then barked at the computer screen. "What? I've given you a biscuit. Are you trying to tell me something?"

"Yes!" cried Josh. "It says; shutting down, well done Harry!" he held up his hand.

Paige turned around and caught a split second glimpse of; PAM IS ONLINE before it vanished. Her hand flew up to her mouth. "Oh my god. I did see that. I'm sure I did." she started typing. "You might not want to speak to me lady, but I want to speak to you."

Harry gave Josh a high five then heard a 'ping' – NEW MESSAGE FROM PAIGE – appeared in the corner of the whirling blue screen. The words knocked Harry back as if they had punched him. Josh gaped at him goggle-eyed.

"Oh no, Harry, *now* what are we going to do?"

Harry, hit re-start then clicked on the message and read aloud;

"Pam, I was worried something bad had happened, I understand if you don't want to talk to me, as long as I know you are alive and well, I promise to leave you alone, love Paige."

"We have to message her back, Josh."

"But, Harry, won't she wonder why it's from us…"

Harry narrowed his eyes. "It won't be from us though, will it, Josh."

"Oh… you mean… pretend to be mum… but what will you say?"

"As little as possible, then she will leave us alone." Harry started typing.

***

Paige was having a girlie night with Ginger, snacking on Iced VoVo biscuits and drinking wine, chatting excitedly in her massive, high spec, state of the art décor – kitchen/diner.

"You got a reply!" Ginger squealed.

"I know, it's amazing!"

"What did she say?! Come on, spill the beans."

"Everything's cool."

"Oh… is that all?"

"U-huh."

"A peculiar thing to say, don't you think?"

Paige let out a reality crashing sigh. "That's what I thought."

"Well, maybe she's young for her age, the fun loving type, like me. You know what they say, life begins at forty." Ginger tried to keep up the positivity.

CHAPTER SIX

SOME KIND OF SPY

Ginger helped herself to a bottle of sauvignon blanc from the fridge. Paige placed a hand over her half empty glass. Ginger shrugged her shoulders.

"Suit yourself, all the more for me." She popped the cork and refilled her own empty glass.

"Don't feel like drinking…" said Paige, scoffing the last iced VoVo. "It'll make me more depressed."

"Oh come on, darl, you got an answer, albeit two words, perhaps she wants to take it slow."

"Perhaps, but her response, it was so… juvenile. I know I haven't seen her since I was three, so it sounds crazy, but *everything's cool* doesn't sound like something my sister would say."

"It could be somebody posing as her, somebody who knows you won the Lotto?"

"That's what I thought."

"Oh darl, I was kidding."

"Wouldn't be the first time, remember that creep, oh, what was his name now?"

"Robin?"

"No, but there's another one, Graham, that was it, all wanting one thing – money."

"A decent self-made man, that's what you need."

"What for? I can't even have children."

"Oh, P, I didn't think, I'm so sorry." Ginger put her wine down and gave Paige a big cuddle.

"It's not that, it's this Pam thing, she's the only family I've got, but I'm hitting a wall. I just want to get to the bottom of it. I mean, it *is* the internet, how do I know it's her?"

"Okay, let's be serious and think about what to do." Ginger looked thoughtful.

"Give up, that's what to do."

"I've got it!" Ginger clicked her fingers. "Why don't you set her up?"

"How do you mean?"

"Make up a story, ask if she remembers it, something that *didn't* happen, and if she says she remembers, then you'll know it's not her."

"G, you my friend are a genius, I knew there was a reason I loved you."

Paige gave her friend a kiss on the cheek and raised her drink. They clinked glasses.

***

Hurrah, the summer holidays. Harry was mucking around with

his rusty old scooter. For the first time since 'it' happened, he and Josh were laughing and having fun.

"This was Dad's scooter, Josh, it's like, ancient. If you fall off, just don't drop it, okay?"

It took Harry right back, watching Josh wobble off, trying and failing to ride, balancing with one leg out. Harry's turn to show off. He rode the scooter down the path like a pro, perfectly balancing one leg out. Josh cheered and clapped as he came whizzing back. Harry took a bow, threw himself on the grass and gazed happily at the clouds floating across the sky.

"We've done it, Joshy."

"What have we done, Harry?"

"Six weeks off, no parents evenings, no sick notes, no more nosey Lurch sticking his beak in, and I can get a job in September when I'm fifteen."

"What about Paige?"

"Oh, that was nothing, she was just going on about a stupid pear tree or something."

"Do you think she'll leave us alone now?"

"No one will say anything now, and if they do, we'll say Mum left us, just like Holley's mum." Harry got up and handed Josh the scooter. "Come on, let's do this." He ran to the end of the path and raised an imaginary flag.

Josh scooted towards Harry, balancing one leg out, for the twentieth time. He successfully reached him without wobbling off. Harry dropped the imaginary flag and cheered, exactly the same way his father had done when he was seven.

"Well done, you did it!"

Josh raised his hand and gave Harry a high five. They didn't perform their special handshake anymore. Ever since the wobbly one they did *that* day, the day they agreed to bury their mum.

"I want a dog for Christmas," Josh blurted, out of breath.

"Crap." Harry looked concerned.

"There won't be, I'll clean up the poo, and feed it, and take it for walks, promise."

"Don't turn around…" said Harry, rubber-necking over his little brother's shoulder.

Josh immediately turned around. Holley was walking up the path. She saw Josh and waved. Numpty waved back. Harry poked him in the ribs. "What did I say, you numbskull."

"You fancy her," Josh teased.

"Shut up, jealous," said Harry, annoyed. Josh let go of the scooter and let it fall to the ground, the disrespectful brat. Harry punched him in the back.

Holley was on the sofa with her head in her hands, crying because her boyfriend had dumped her. She loved cats, so Harry showed her a funny cat video on his iPhone, but she cried even more. Not having the first clue how to stop a girl crying, he made her a drink of squash instead, while his little brother handed her a toilet roll with one sheet of paper on it. It was the last sheet as well. Stupid Josh.

"Thanks, guys." Holley blew her nose.

Harry waited until big ears had sprawled himself safely in front of the telly, so he could talk to Holley in private and console her like a mature grown-up.

"He's a two-timing jock, and a big head."

"Everyone says that, I wish he was more like you…" said Holley, giving him a coy smile.

Harry, looked at his watch. "Anyway, umm…"

"I know, you've got loads to do, I feel better now anyway, and my dad will wonder where I am, he's so overprotective, it drives me crazy."

"I get the feeling your dad doesn't like me much."

"Don't take it personally, he's always been like that, he can't get over investigating everything, just because he used to be in the Met…"

Harry gulped. "You mean, *the* Met, as in police Met."

"Yeah, he reckons he's some kind of spy." Holley guzzled her squash and put the glass down. "I better go, thanks for the chat, and the drink, and the toilet roll… sheet." She chuckled.

Poor Harry, he wanted to but he couldn't, he watched helplessly as Holley made her way to the front door. Josh stared at him like he was dense. "Go on," he urged.

"Holley, wait!" Harry leapt off the sofa and ran into the hall. The front door creaked as she turned the handle. "Holley, I just… well, it's just…"

Screw the talking. Harry's ill-timed kiss just so happened to coincide with her opening the door. They both jumped back, startled. There was Professor Evans, with his fist poised mid-air.

"Hello, boys… and girl, sorry, didn't mean to surprise you, a quick word with your mum, if I may, please Harry."

"She's um… ill, Professor, sorry," Harry stammered.

"I thought you said she was at work?" said Holley.

"She is… she's ill, at work."

"When will she be back?" the professor grilled.

"I don't know, Professor." Harry swallowed nervously. "She said she might work late today."

"Right, I'll pop back, in say, an hour?"

"Two would be better… or tomorrow, would be better still?"

"See you in two hours, Harry." The professor saluted and sauntered off.

Harry closed the door, leant against it and sighed. "Bugger." Holley eyed him questioningly.

Josh shot out of the lounge, talking at the same time. "We'd better think of something, Harry, otherwise he's going to find out Mum's gone to…" Josh gawked at Holley as the word rolled off his tongue, "…heaven."

Harry felt sick.

***

Paige was on her computer staring at the message from Pam, shaking her head in disbelief at yet another juvenile response. It simply said;

"Yeah, I remember, I ate all the pears, ha, ha, it was fun."

"Fun was it, Pam?" she said out loud to herself. "I don't recall you eating all the fruit off Mum and Dad's prize pear tree. We never had a prize pear tree…"

***

Harry finished off his confession to Holley, "…so we buried her in the garden."

"You buried your mum in the garden?"

"Yes."

"Just like that?"

"Mm-hmm."

"Why do boys always lie?"

"It's not a lie," Josh defended Harry.

"I heard what you said, Josh."

"What did I say?"

Holley rolled her eyes. "She's gone to Devon."

"I said heaven, not Devon!"

"Stop lying! I saw her in the garden the other day…" Holley walked over to the window. "Standing right there." She pointed directly to the newly grown grass patch.

Josh stared at Harry open-mouthed. Holley placed her hands on her hips. "I know what I saw."

"Impossible." Harry shook his head.

Holley threw her arms into the air. "Alright, have it your way, you buried her in the garden, that's a terrible thing to say, let alone do."

"I know," said Harry, full of remorse.

"I really should tell my dad…" Holley scolded.

Josh threw himself onto the floor and curled into a ball. Harry hung his head in shame.

"However, I would have done exactly the same thing in your shoes."

Josh unravelled himself. "You… you would?" he stuttered.

"Hell yeah, I know what it's like to lose a mum. Mine's got a new family now, she doesn't speak to us anymore. If I lost my dad I'd have nobody." She turned to Harry. "If I had a little sister I'd want to protect her too."

"Does this mean… you're not going to tell your dad?" Harry dared to ask, inhaling a deep breath.

"No… I'm not. I'm not going to tell anyone, your secret is safe with me."

Harry remembered to exhale. Mammoth relief washed over him.

"I don't know how long you will get away with it though… Professor Evans is coming back…" Holley looked at her watch. "In one hour, thirty-five minutes and ten seconds."

***

Paige was on the phone, having a heart to heart with Ginger, strutting up and down the wooden veranda, running her hands through her hair and wearing her slippers out.

"Who the bloody hell have I been speaking to? And why are they pretending to be her?"

"There's one way to find out."

"I'm not doing that."

"You know, Qantas are very good with nervous passengers."

"Wild horses couldn't get me on an aeroplane."

"I'll come with you! I mean, I understand your fear of cars, after the crash and losing your parents and everything, but flying darl, it's the safest way to travel."

"No way, thanks G, but it'll only lead to heartache, there's no point, we obviously weren't destined to find each other, end of."

***

Josh was crouching down, spying out of the bedroom window. "He's coming!"

Harry galloped down the stairs. There was a rat-a-tat-tat on the front door. He calmly opened it. "Oh, hi Professor, hang on… Mu-um! Professor Evans is here! Are you out the shower yet?"

The sound of cascading water radiated from upstairs. "No, I'm not!" called a faint female voice.

The professor was taken aback. He raised his hand in a leaving gesture. "Sorry, Pammie… Mrs Jones!" he shouted.

A woman, with a towel wrapped around her body, a turban towel on her head, wearing Gucci sunglasses, beamed and waved at him from upstairs. The embarrassed professor gave a feeble wave back.

"Sorry to interrupt, I hope you're feeling better soon, see you some other time."

"Goodbye Professor." Harry closed the door and gave a double thumbs-up to the imposter on the landing. He tore back up the stairs. Holley, removed the sunglasses. He gazed at her pretty face, she gazed back at him. There was a moment between them...

"Oh shoot! I'd better put my clothes back on." She rushed off into the bathroom.

Harry pried open the bedroom curtains to make sure the coast was clear. To his horror, just as the professor was strolling away, Lurch was striding up the path.

"Professor! What on earth are you doing here?" Harry overhead.

"I popped round to see Mrs Jones, if that's alright with you?"

"And did you?"

"Did I what?"

"Did you see Mrs Jones?"

"Yes, I did see her."

Lurch mumbled something in response but Harry couldn't hear, he was too busy talking to himself, willing the professor to leave. "Please, please, go away," he begged. The professor walked off and got into his car. Phew, that was a close call.

"Who go away?" said a female voice behind him.

"Holley, your dad's here! Quick, go!" said Harry, shoving her out of the room. They sped down the stairs, Harry opened the front door.

"Dad," smiled Holley, stepping outside. "I was just coming."

"You should have been home hours ago," Lurch said, "A quick word with your mother please, chap?"

"She's at work..." said Harry.

"She's ill..." said Holley, simultaneously.

"Really?!" Lurch grabbed Holley by the arm. "We're going home and you're not to come round here anymore!" he marched her away.

Closing the door, Harry noticed the professor sitting in his car, snooping. He started the engine and slowly drove away.

Half an hour later, Harry's phone rang. It was a facetime call from Holley.

"Hi, you okay?" said Harry, feeling incredibly guilty.

"No," said Holley, lying on her bed and frowning at the screen. "What do you think of this?" She switched the screen view and panned the phone around to show Harry her beautifully decorated girlie bedroom.

"Nice… if you like pink." Harry grinned.

"I did, when I was ten, and my dad wasn't a moaning old misery guts…" Holley switched the screen back to her. "This will be my prison for the rest of the holidays. I've been grounded."

"My bad, that's all my fault."

"Nah, it's not your fault, it's my dad. He's been like this ever since my mum left us…" she lowered her voice, "I'm not allowed to speak to you, so I have to be quiet in case he's spying outside my door."

"Holley, thanks for what you did, I really appreciate it, and… I know I don't act like I do, but I do – really like you."

"I like you too…" Holley giggled. "And don't worry, I promise not to tell anyone your mum's gone to Devon," she whispered.

"Listen, Holley, about that…"

"What was that?"

"What was what?"

"I heard a noise outside my bedroom door." Holley lowered her voice to a murmur. "I've got to go, sorry, bye."

The screen went black.

***

Harry opened the front door and breathed in the crisp autumn air. Six weeks had passed since the professor and Lurch incident and no one had said a dickie bird. All in all, it could only mean one thing – they had gotten away with it.

"Come on, bud, or we'll be late."

His partner in crime emerged, all dressed up ready for the new school term in his freshly laundered uniform and pressed shirt. Harry felt a glow of pride. He had become a dab hand at ironing these days.

"Is this really going to be fresh start, Harry?"

"Yep, I've got an interview at the market later, we can start to put all this behind us now."

Miss Allen was busy marking at her desk. The classroom was so quiet you could almost hear a pin drop. Everyone had their heads down studying, everyone that is, except Harry, who had a watchful eye on an older pupil who had come in and whispered something in the teacher's ear, then left.

"Harry Jones?" Miss Allen beckoned for him to go over and see her.

Damn it. He had a sneaking suspicion that was going to happen.

Harry made his way to the headmaster's office, cracking his knuckles, worrying and wondering. He hadn't heard a word from Holley all holiday. What if she'd told her dad and he'd told the professor? No, she wouldn't do that, Harry was sure of it… kind of.

Josh was already there, waiting outside, leaning against the wall, biting his nails. "What's going on Harry, I can hear the professor talking to someone?"

Harry pinned his ear to the door. He overheard the professor on the phone.

"Mrs Jones didn't make it for parents evening… did she attend the year seven assembly… she didn't… what about the harvest festival… she didn't go to that either… hmm…"

"What's he saying, Harry?"

Before Harry had a chance to answer, the professor opened the door.

"Ah, boys, do come on in…" he ushered them inside. "Bear with me for a moment, I just need to finish my notes, then you'll have my undivided attention…"

Josh looked at Harry, his eyes woefully wide. Harry discreetly lifted a finger to his lips and stared at the vast collage of children's drawings of aliens and planets that adorned most of the walls, desperately trying to think of a way out of the situation. Maybe he could say his mum was abducted by aliens? No, that was a dumb idea. The professor coughed and put his pen down.

"It's all rather mysterious, isn't it, boys?" he said.

"It's year three's interpretation of life beyond our universe, isn't it sir?" said Harry.

"I'm not talking about the wall art, Harry."

"What do you mean sir?" asked Harry, praying he sounded more nonchalant than he actually felt.

"I wasn't born yesterday…" said the professor, staring at Harry, his beady eyes boring straight into his soul. "In fact, I wasn't born long after the dinosaurs, there's not a lot that gets past me…" he narrowed his eyes. "It's time for you to confess, boys…"

Harry's mouth had completely dried up, he felt sick to the pit of his stomach and his heart was beating in rhythm and almost as loud as the ticking clock on the wall.

"I'm waiting?" said the stern professor.

Josh, too petrified to speak, turned his lie-hiding squinty-eyes to face Harry.

"Alright alright, but please professor, don't blame Josh, it wasn't his fault," Harry pleaded.

"I can't let you take the blame, Harry, I don't care what happens." Bold as brass, Josh faced the professor. "It wasn't him, it was both of us."

There was a moment of uneasy silence, apart from the ominous sound of the ticking clock, as Harry and Josh, like sitting ducks, awaited their fate.

"Oh, I can see that! You've consistently failed to hand in any homework, both of you!"

"Did you say… homework, sir?" said Harry, turning to Josh, whose eyes were now wide open and staring back at him.

"Indeed I did. We have high standards at this school and you two have been consistent in your lack of homework."

Gargantuan amounts of relief swamped Harry. "I'm sorry sir, we will do it from now on, all of it, won't we, Josh?"

"Oh yes sir, we definitely will!" Josh piped up.

"No more excuses, otherwise I will be getting your mother in here…" The professor scanned Harry's face for a reaction. His blank expression gave nothing away. "By the way, how is your mum? I didn't get to speak to her properly at the start of the holidays. Is she better?"

"No," said Harry.

"Yes," said Josh, simultaneously.

The professor leaned forward across the desk, and clasped his hands together. "I don't know what's going on, boys, but you've got until tomorrow lunchtime to come clean, or I'm going to the police."

CHAPTER SEVEN

PARTNERS IN CRIME

Harry wandered aimlessly around the noisy playground. His stomach churned as he racked his empty brain to come up with a solution. Josh was not helping, freaking out and badgering him with der-brain questions.

"What are we going to do, Harry? Are we going to go to prison? Shall we run away, Harry?"

"I'll think of something, Josh, give me some space, go and play with your friends."

"I can't Harry, I feel sick. I don't want to go to prison."

Harry stopped aimlessly wandering and put his hands on Josh's shoulders. "You have to trust me on this, I will fix it, but we have to try and act normal, okay?"

"Okay, Harry."

Whatever you say Harry. Three bags full Harry. He would jump off a cliff if Harry told him to. Harry watched as Josh ran off and joined in a game of tag, trying to act normal, the poor kid. The weight of responsibility on Harry's shoulders was unbearable, this was all his stupid fault. He had buried his mum and ruined his little brother's life.

Someone tapped him on the shoulder. Harry spun round to see Holley with a cheesy grin on her face. "Have we met? My name's Rapunzel, I've been trapped in a 1980's pink tower for over a month..."

Harry was too preoccupied with his own problems to get the joke. There was a moment of apprehensive silence, until they both attempted to speak at the same time.

"Harry, I think my dad knows..."

"Holley, I know you don't believe..."

Holley chuckled. "Sorry... you go first."

"I need to tell you something, about my mum..."

"Harry, wherever she is, it's no one's business, my dad interrogated me this morning but I didn't say a word. If Poirot thinks grounding me for the whole bloody summer's the answer, he's more stupid than I thought."

"I'm sorry you got grounded..." Harry felt bad, that was all his stupid fault too. This could be his last chance to make it up to the girl he had fallen in love with. "How about we go to the open cinema tonight, *Day of the Dead's* on?"

"Harry, I really like you but..." Holley stopped. She'd seen something over his shoulder.

Harry turned around to see her cooler than cool, arrogant, two-timing jock of a bighead ex-boyfriend, Sid from sixth-form looming towards them.

"Hey, Jonesy, what you doing talking to my girl?" he put his arms around Holley and squeezed her tight. The school bell shrieked. "Later, babe." Sid kissed Holley full on the lips. "*Day of the Dead* tonight, be ready at six," he winked, then pointed an imaginary gun at Harry as he strutted off.

Holley squirmed with embarrassment.

"You really like me, but… you're going with him," said Harry, choking on his words.

Holley didn't say anything, she didn't need to. Her red face said it all. Harry was crestfallen. Holley was back with Sid the snake, Lurch was on his case, and the professor was going to the police tomorrow at lunchtime. Could things get any worse?

***

Paige squeezed her eyes shut tight and crossed her heart as the aeroplane wheels bumped onto the tarmac, taxied along the runway and came to an abrupt stop. The captain's voice crackled over the tannoy.

"Ladies and gentlemen thank you for flying with us today. On behalf of Qantas airlines I'd like to wish you a safe and pleasant onward journey."

***

Harry hadn't slept a wink all night. Josh was still in his pyjamas, curled into a ball on the bedroom floor. Harry paced around him in circles, cracking his knuckles. "Today's the day, we have to confess, Josh, before the professor goes to the police."

Josh unravelled himself. "No Harry! We can't! They'll put us in an orphanage! Or put us in prison! You said you would fix it!"

"We don't have any choice, Josh! Don't you get it? We're done for! It's over!"

"Wait!" Josh had a glint in his eye. "Harry, I've got an idea!"

***

It wasn't even winter in the UK and she was freezing. Paige wasn't used to this Ice Age temperature of seven degrees Celsius. She finished her wake-me-up coffee, unzipped her suitcase and pulled out a hat and scarf. Wrapping herself up nice and warm, she made her way out of the terminal and hailed a taxi.

***

Josh's idea was the only idea. Yes, it meant leaving lots of stuff behind but – a PlayStation versus a prison sentence – no competition. Harry rushed around, frantically stuffing his clothes into a backpack, as did Josh, until they heard a loud knock on the front door. Josh gawped at him. Harry placed a finger to his lips and looked out of the bedroom window.

"It's Holley," said Harry, surprised.

***

"Can you take me to this address please?" Paige handed the taxi driver a piece of paper and climbed into the back of the cab.

"So, what part of New Zealand you from?" quizzed the driver as he drove away.

"A little place called Australia." Paige grinned, British people; so funny.

"Oh, you're an Aussie, sorry." he laughed. "You all sound the same to me."

***

"Why aren't you in school?" asked Holley.

"Why aren't *you* in school?" Harry replied, holding the door open an inch.

"Because I've been looking for you! Harry, I saw my dad walking across the playground with the professor."

"What, why?"

Holley sighed. "He overheard our conversation that day, about your mum being in Devon. I told him she's not but he doesn't believe me. Harry, I don't know how to say this, but, well, I think she's met someone else and living with another family, like my mum."

"What are you talking about?"

"She's still around Harry, I've seen her, in your garden. And I've seen her sitting on the church step at the graveyard, she looked upset. I think she feels bad for leaving you."

"Holley, my mum's dead…"

"Harry, my mum's dead to me too… look, I understand how you feel, I haven't come here to give you a lecture, I've come to warn you, my dad said at breakfast that he's going to the police."

***

"So, what brings you here from the other side of the world? It's a long old way to come," said the taxi driver, making friendly conversation.

"I'm visiting my sister."

"Ah, a family reunion, nice, how was the flight?"

"Twenty-two hours long," Paige yawned, "and I spent the whole time with my eyes closed listening to my hypnosis CD trying to sleep and forget about it."

"Your sister must be one special lady, wild horses wouldn't get me on a plane for that long."

"Ha! Famous last words, that's exactly what I said to my best friend."

"Oh well, you're here now, love, the worst is over," smiled the driver.

***

Harry looked at his watch, it was past lunchtime, which was the professor's deadline for going to the police. That's if he hadn't gone already, knowing the boys hadn't showed up for school, and especially after speaking with Lurch. They could turn up any minute. It was all such a mess, they had to get out of there fast. Harry flew up the stairs to see how Josh was getting on.

"Hurry up, Josh, take the bare minimum, we'll get a taxi to the train station then..."

Harry was disturbed by another loud bang on the front door. He crept over to the window.

"It's a woman?" he whispered, peeping through the glass.

A voice called through the letter box. "Hello? Anybody home?"

"It sounds like the Crocodile Dundee woman!" Josh whispered as he pigeon-stepped over to the window and spied out. The woman looked up.

"Harry, she looks like Mum!"

"Oh no!" Harry whispered. "It must be... Paige!"

"HELLO?" shouted the Australian voice.

"How did she find us, Harry?"

"God knows, some nosey neighbour probably."

"What are we going to do?"

"Let her in, pretend Mum's at work, talk to her for a bit, then sneak out the back door, okay?"

"Okay, Harry."

The front door opened. Paige gasped and dropped her handbag. "Oh my God! You must be..." her hand flew up to her mouth. "You look just like my sister!"

Paige followed Harry and Josh into the lounge, dragging her suitcase behind her, she looked around the room ever so slightly disgusted. "Ugh... squalor."

"What does that mean?" asked Josh.

"It means, I had higher hopes for your mother's standards of living."

Josh grimaced. "You talk funny."

"Josh. Don't be rude," Harry retorted.

Paige laughed. "That's alright…" adopting an English accent she continued. "Would one prefer one to talk like this?"

Josh stared at her aghast. "Hey, that's really good."

"Well, I was born in England you know, when did you say your mum gets in from work?"

"Um… later?" Harry offered.

"I hope she won't be too shocked to see me?"

"She won't!" said Josh, excited. "She talked about you all the time, didn't she, Harry!"

"Yes, Josh, she DOES." Harry glared at him.

"Do you have a spare room?" Paige enquired.

"What for?" asked Harry.

"So I can freshen up, empty my case, I was hoping to stay for a bit. Oz to the UK, it's not exactly a day trip, I need to chill, that journey almost killed me. I wouldn't be much good to your mum if I was dead, now would I?"

Paige bumped her suitcase up the stairs. The boys followed her closely. She turned the handle to their mum's bedroom.

"NO!" Harry shouted. "I mean… no, you can't go in there, that's Mum's room," he said, trying to sound casual.

Too late. Paige opened the door. There it was, the shrine, exactly the same as it was that awful day. Harry had gone in there with a black bin bag and tiptoed out of the room, never to go in there again. There were no curtains, just an untidy sheet on the bed and unopened boxes everywhere. It was cold and had a musty stench.

"Ew... I can't believe your mother sleeps in here, it's revolting."

Paige noticed the picture of her and their mum on the bedside table. "Oh my." She made a beeline for it, picked it up and smiled. "I have the same picture on my bedside locker too." She put it back down carefully and spotted the spilt pot of pills on the floor next to the bed.

"Moron!" Josh murmured to Harry.

Paige bent down and picked up the empty pill pot. "Who's a moron?"

"You're the moron, big mouth!" Harry glared at Josh.

"What are these spilt pills all about? What on earth has happened to my sister?"

***

Paige stood on the newly grown grass patch, the old opening to the secret den where their mum was buried. Harry had told her the whole story. She knelt down and stroked the grass, tears streamed down her face. "No matter what happens to us, Pam, always know, wherever you are, we are sisters and we will find each other, I promise..."

Gutted, Harry and Josh remained motionless.

"I knew something was wrong, if only I had got through to her sooner, poor Pam..." Paige looked at the boys, heartbroken. "I do get it, I understand why you did what you did."

"Can you help us?" Josh begged.

"Josh, I cannot condone what you have done, what you've done is so bad. It's too harrowing for words."

Harry hung his head in shame. "I know."

"How could you do such a terrible thing, Harry?"

Josh burst into tears. "He did it to protect me! To stop them taking me away!"

Harry didn't know what to say. He just stood there in silence, shivering in the cold, huddled together with Josh. Paige let out a sigh and studied the sky as if searching for an answer. A shaft of heavenly light cascaded down on them. It was a moment before she spoke again.

"No, there's no excuse, Josh is a kid, but you're old enough to know better Harry…"

Harry waited, quietly dreading what she had to say next.

"You have to hand yourselves in to the police. Do you understand?"

Harry nodded in agreement, he was ready to meet his doom. He'd known all along, deep down, that this day would come.

"Don't blame Harry, it's not his fault! It's all my fault!" Josh defended him.

"No, she's right, Josh."

"Go inside, wait for me in the lounge, I want a few minutes alone, then I'm taking you both straight to the police station."

Tired and defeated, Harry knew the game was over, he bowed his head in disgrace and slowly walked away, dragging his heavy feet.

"Where are you going?" Josh raced after him and grabbed his arm. "You're not listening to her, are you?"

Harry, like a programmed robot, did as he was told. Josh followed him into the lounge.

"Let's go upstairs and grab the backpacks, she's in the garden, we can sneak out the front door! Like you said, Harry!" Josh tugged at his sleeve and shook his arm violently. "Harry?!"

Harry couldn't move, he felt like he was stuck in glue. Josh slapped his face. That did it. Harry suddenly came to his senses and snapped out of his pitiful trance.

"Why am I standing in here like a bonehead?"

"I don't know! This is our chance, Harry!"

"This *is* our chance… this is our last chance, isn't it?!"

"Yes! Der! Come on!"

"Let's go, Josh, quick!"

Harry tore up the stairs, with Josh hot-footing behind him. He zipped up his backpack. Josh zipped up his. Another loud thump on the door resonated up the stairs. Harry stared at his brother with dread then rushed over to the window. A police car was parked outside the gate.

"Too late, the police are here, Josh…" Harry dropped his backpack onto the floor. Josh dropped his. Harry put an arm around his little brother's shoulders and pulled him close.

"It's game over, buddy."

Hand in hand, partners in crime, Harry and Josh walked solemnly to the front door.

"Harry I'm scared!"

Harry squeezed his brother's hand gently and winked. "Don't be scared, Josh, be strong…"

"Harry, I don't want us to be split up! What if we never see each other again?" Tears spilled onto Josh's cheeks.

Harry wiped his little brother's tears away with his cuff. "No matter what happens to us, Josh, always know, wherever you are, we are brothers, we will find each other, I promise…"

Harry felt strangely comforted knowing Josh would have a new family, a better family, the poor little kid deserved one. It was Harry's stupid idea to bury their mum, and it was Harry who should face the consequences. So be it. He opened the door. Professor Evans, Lurch, and two police officers were standing there.

"Is this the Jones' residence?" said the policeman.

"Yes," said Harry.

"What's your name, son?" the policewoman asked.

"I'm Harry Jones, this is my brother, Josh."

"We need to speak to your mother, Pamela Jones, is she here?" enquired the policeman.

"No, she's not," Harry confessed.

"I bloody well knew it!" exclaimed Lurch.

"Son, it's time for you to tell the truth, where is your mother?" the policewoman quizzed.

The charade was finally over. Harry took a sharp intake of breath, mentally preparing himself for the godawful thing he was about to say next.

"She's in the garden... buried..."

The two police officers, the professor and Lurch stared at him in horror. It was like the world had stopped revolving...

"Under a ton of brambles!" called an English female voice.

Harry twisted his head around to see Paige, carrying a pair of pruning scissors, marching towards them. She put her arms lovingly around the boy's shoulders and smiled.

"What's happening here, then? Everything alright, officers?"

"I... um... we... um," the policeman stammered and turned to Lurch. "Can you confirm that this the boy's mother?"

"I've never met the woman, but he has." He pointed at the professor.

The police officers and Lurch were eye-balling the professor, awaiting an answer. The professor stared at Paige intently. Her face was smiling but Harry could see the desperation in her eyes. There was a tense uneasy silence. Finally the professor spoke.

"Indeed it is," he said.

"Lovely to see you, again." Paige shook the professor's hand.

"Sorry, I've been keeping a low profile for a while, the boys have been keeping a very big secret, haven't you boys?"

Harry turned to Paige. "Oh no, you're not going to tell them now, are you?"

"Yes, Harry, I have to… I didn't want to tell, but… I've had a mini face lift. It caused a lot of bruising, I had to go into hiding. It's not the sort of hideous thing you want people to see."

The professor suppressed a smile. Lurch squirmed with embarrassment.

"Ooh, looks good." The policewoman waggled her head in that understanding female way. "You've got a lovely tan as well, hasn't she?" she said, turning to her colleague.

The cringing policeman nodded and took his hat off. "Sorry to have troubled you, ma'am."

"That's quite alright, thanks for your concern, now if you'll excuse us, we've got a lot to sort out, haven't we, boys?"

Harry and Josh were speechless. So too were the police officers, the professor and Lurch as they humbly backed away. Paige smiled sweetly, and closed the door.

"Does this mean… you're not going to tell the police?" asked Harry.

"It means, Harry, we've got a bit of breathing space, to make a plan."

"But… you're not our mum," said Josh.

"But I am your aunt, Josh, and you're my nephews, we're family, and families stick together. I've got a lot of money boys, and a lot of contacts. I will wangle something if I can, but if I can't, you'll have to hand yourselves in, and goddammit, so will I. Do you understand?"

Harry and Josh nodded in stunned silence.

***

It was a beautiful cold frosty December morning. A taxi pulled up outside the cottage and its horn beeped. The cottage door opened. Paige, Harry and Josh stepped out pulling their suitcases. All three of them were dressed in woolly hats, gloves and scarves. For the first time in a long time the boys were well dressed, healthy and happy. Paige exhaled a breath of crisp winter air and put her arms around their shoulders.

"Right boys, are you ready for the land down under, 29 degrees and Christmas on the beach?"

The boys gazed up at the SOLD board and grinned at each other.

"You in brother?" asked Josh.

"Oh, I'm in definitely in, brother," laughed Harry.

They high-fived, then did the special handshake.

~ EPILOGUE ~

Everything was epic in that land down under.

Paige's house was hugely epic. Their new shared bedroom (the boys had insisted on being together) was crazily epic with all the latest games consoles and a wall-mounted 72-inch TV. And Paige's pool was epic, too.

Harry liked to sit on the edge of it, his feet dangling in the water, and think of his dear mum as he gazed at the pool's stunning centerpiece – a beautiful fountain featuring three huge koi carp with water spouting from their mouths.

The same fountain that was now in the garden back in England. Before they left for Oz, Paige had told them she was worried that whoever bought the cottage might unearth their secret if they decided to do any digging. Or, worse still, what if the old pit collapsed and the new owner unearthed a fright?

She wasn't lying when she said she had plenty of money. No expense spared, Paige had the entire garden landscaped, concreted over, paved, walls built, seating areas, a fire pit, a barbecue pit, and a replica of the fountain from back home stood proud in the middle.

"No one will want to change this," she'd said, "it's beautiful, just like my sister and my boys."

It had been a crisp and frosty day when they'd lit that fire pit, and the barbecue. Paige had put Harry in charge of cooking the burgers and sausages. Harry had felt, for the first time, like a real grown up that day as Holley watched him cook and then told him how delicious it was. She'd kissed him on the lips before she went home. And soon, Holley was coming to visit in the holidays, all paid for by Paige.

Something else Paige did – before the landscaping took place – something Harry doesn't like to think about too much. She'd hired a concrete mixer, bought enough mix to fill in the old pit. Harry and his brother, along with Holley, had been sent into town with enough money to visit McDonald's (twice), Nando's (once), see three movies at the cinema, take an open-top bus tour *and* enjoy a scary ghost walk, with the orders to *stay away all day*. Paige had been exhausted when they'd got home. All the mix was gone. The pit had been filled. No risk of collapse. The boys had flung themselves at her, despite how mucky she was, and they'd all cried together. Paige truly was epic, just like Mum.

And speaking of ghost walks. Face-timing Holley every day, she insists she can see dead people. When she comes for her visit, Harry has plans to take her to the local graveyard. It's old and spooky and, well, he's pictured it many times, Holley's lips on his, in the graveyard. Maybe that will be a story for another day.

~ **THE END** ~

THANK YOU!

To my amazing preditor, John Hudspith – for being much more than 'just' an editor, thank you for forcing me to explore the unknown world of POV and not giving up on me when I tried to cheat ☺

To my fantastically brilliant cover creator, my better half, Oliver Martin – for breathing life into my ideas for cover design.

My beta readers, Teri Coffey, Lisa Edwards and Tracy Jordan – thank you for believing in me, your inspiring words, and great ideas.

Special thanks to Tony Jordan, for being the sole reason I put pen to paper in the first place.

~~~~~~~

Printed in Great Britain
by Amazon